Utterly Me, Clarice Bean

For Sylv
Utterly
Thank You

First U.S. paperback edition 2005

First published in Great Britain in 2002 by Orchard Books, London

The Library of Congress has cataloged the hardcover edition as follows:
Child, Lauren.
Utterly me, Clarice Bean / Lauren Child. —1st U.S. ed.
p.   cm.
Summary: When someone steals the winner's trophy for the school book project,
Clarice emulates her favorite book heroine, Ruby Redfort the detective.
ISBN 0-7636-2186-2 (hardcover)
[1. Schools—Fiction. 2. Contests—Fiction. 3. Family life—Fiction.
4. Humorous stories. 5. Mystery and detective stories.] I. Title.
PZ7.C4383Ut2003
[Fic]—dc21   2002041528

ISBN 0-7636-2788-7 (paperback)

4 6 8 10 9 7 5

Printed in the United States of America

This book was typeset in M Bembo.

Candlewick Press
2067 Massachusetts Avenue
Cambridge, Massachusetts 02140

visit us at www.candlewick.com

Utterly Me, Clarice Bean

Lauren Child

CANDLEWICK PRESS
CAMBRIDGE, MASSACHUSETTS

Chapter 1

This is me, Clarice Bean.

I am not an only child, but I sometimes wish I was.

My family is six people, which is sometimes too many.

Not always, just sometimes.

My dad is mostly in an office on the phone, going, "I can't talk now—I'm up to my ears in it."

Mom is always gribbling about pants on the floor and shoes on the sofa.

She says, "This house doesn't clean itself, you know.

"Who do you think does everything around here?

"Mr. Nobody?

"I don't get paid to pick up your smelly socks! If I did, I'd be a rich woman." etc. etc. non stop.

I am the third oldest, and I think it would have been a good idea if I was the youngest, too.

I am not quite sure why my mom and dad wanted to have more children after me.

They don't need another one and it's a shame because he is spoiling it for everyone else.

He is called Minal Cricket and he tends to be utterly a nuisance.

He is nonstop whining and causing other people to get themselves in trouble.

You might think
it would be a
relief to come to school,
but if you do,
then obviously you don't know
some of the people in my class.
Naming no names,
i.e., Grace Grapello,
what a showoff.

Sometimes I stare boredly into space,
thinking **utterly** of
nothing.
This makes Mrs. Wilberton very irritated.

I get on her nerves.

I know this because she is always telling me I do.

To be honest, Mrs. Wilberton is not my favorite person on the planet of Earth.

Unfortunately, I am from Earth and she is my teacher.

Mrs. Wilberton says I have got utterly not a speck of concentration.

I am trying to prove her wrong about this by trying to remember to concentrate.

I think about it all the time. I am so desperately trying *not* to not concentrate and I say to myself, *Don't drift off like you did yesterday.* And then I start thinking about how I drifted off yesterday and how I was thinking I must listen to Mrs. Wilberton and all the things she is telling me.

And then I am wondering,

How does all this stuff she is telling me fit into my head?

And then I am wondering if I should have a clear-out of the stuff I don't need anymore—

you know,

like when my dad cleared out the attic,

except we all decided

we needed

everything

and he just had to put it all back again.

But maybe valuable space is being taken up in

my

head

with not the important things and

that

　　is why

　　　I can't

concentrate

because all my concentration space

　　has been used up

on things like

"Elbows off the table"

　　　　　　and

"Don't pinch your brother"
　　　　and

pointless

not needed

things

that

don't matter.

"CLARICE

Will
you
please
come
back
down
to
Earth

It's Mrs. Wilberton.

You

can

tell

by

her

honking

goose

voice.

She says,

"Clarice Bean,
you are utterly lacking in the
concentration department.
A common housefly has got
more ability to apply itself!"

And I want to say,

"You are utterly lacking in the
manners department, Mrs. Wilberton,
and a rhinoceros has got more
politeness than you."

But I don't say it because Mrs. Wilberton is allowed to say rude things about me and I am not allowed to say them back.

Those are the rules of school.

Then Mrs. Wilberton says, "Class, I am announcing the very exciting subject of this year's parents' night competition."

Mrs. Wilberton doesn't look one bit excited but I think it would take an elephant running into the classroom waving its arms around to get Mrs. Wilberton hopping.

Anyway, everybody must pair up and think of an exhibit that they would like to put together and have on show for when all the parents traipse in to see just what their little darlings have been up to.

Of course, me and Betty Moody are a pair because we are utterly best friends.

Mrs. Wilberton says the project must be based on a book we have read and learned something from.

It sounds *utterly dreary to me.*

When I get home, I go straight upstairs to Mom's closet.

I take a mini cheese with me because they are my favorite things at the moment, and you never know when you might want something to nibble.

Mom's closet is a good place to be on your own by yourself.

And it's where I like to read my book.

You need a flashlight and it is lucky that I got one for Christmas.

I had to ask for it and put a note up the chimney for Santa Claus.

I don't think I believe in Santa Claus but Mom and Dad want me to, so I write to him anyway.

I wrote, "Dear Santa Claus, If you are true, please can I have a flashlight, and if you are not true, then please can someone else get me one?"

I think it is important to keep your options

open, because you never know what is the actual in fact truth these days.

Granny says the world is a very mysterious place, what with men in space and so on.

She says, "After all, who would have thought you would one day be able to send someone a picture down the telephone, or cook a leg of lamb in five minutes?"

I didn't used to be so much of a reader, it just happened when Granny gave me a book called THERE WAS A GIRL NAMED RUBY. Mom says there and then I turned into a bookworm.

THERE WAS A GIRL NAMED RUBY is from a whole series of books called THE RUBY REDFORT COLLECTION.

Betty Moody and me utterly love them.

They are about this amazing girl—she's a bit like a detective but she's only eleven.

She doesn't have any brothers and sisters and gets to go on these sort of adventures.

The
most
I
do
is
go
to
the
corner
store
on
my
own.

Ruby Redfort lives in this crazy sort of house and her parents are fabulously rich and she has an actual butler man who gets to do all these things for her.

He's called Hitch, which is his last name.

You only get to call butlers by their last name—it's normal in the world of butlers.

Ruby Redfort drives to school in a helicopter sometimes, and has these gadgets and things.

Even Ruby Redfort's sports gear isn't normal. Her sneakers have special springing power so she can jump over her enemies, and her bathing suit has a built-in propeller so she can swim as fast as a mackerel.

Ruby gets mail all her own—imagine that!

It's all interesting and top-secret from other detectives and government presidents and people, and it is full of clues in strange codes.

But no one ever suspects anything, because why would they?

That's the most ingenious thing about Ruby

Redfort: she doesn't need a disguise because who would expect a schoolgirl to be a master investigator agent?

No one, that's who!

I only get mail at birthdays, so I've started sending off for things.

There are lots of free things you can get them to send you if you fill out the coupons.

Mom calls it junk mail but I think it's interesting to get mail, even if it is about thermal undershirts.

My dad gets mail with

PRIVATE

written on it,

so for all I know he is a secret agent himself.

I have had a sneak peek at one of the letters and there were lots of numbers and dates and then some words in red saying

FINAL REMINDER.

It's all utterly suspicious.

And the other day, Dad said that
"There might be a reshuffle going on at work"
    and that he
        "will have to jump through hoops"
if he wants to get
    "a share of the pie."
He says, "The big cheese has been making noises
and some people might be left out in the cold if

they don't keep their
eye on the ball.
But that's the
way the cookie
crumbles."
I'm not sure what he
was talking about.
Betty Moody says it
is probably almost
definitely code.

Dad says, "I can assure you that if I was a secret agent, I would go and be secret somewhere hot and sunny with a nice beach and no telephones."

Dad usually has to have a telephone with him at all times. He utterly mustn't be uncontactable for even a second.

It would be very hard for me to be a secret agent because my whole family is always poking their noses into my private affairs and to do anything secretly is extremely impossible.

Betty says you need to have a good cover story and gadgets, which are disguised as other everyday objects.

Like i.e. for example, Ruby Redfort's toaster also converts into a special fax machine.

If you press the button
d
o
w
n,
a secret message
gets transmitted from Ruby's boss at HQ and

is written
onto the
toast.

And then after Ruby Redfort has read it, she can just eat the evidence so no one will ever see it.

Betty also says, "You must be confident as a cucumber in order not to arouse suspicion."

Ruby's parents know utterly nothing about her secret life as a mystery solver and special agent because Ruby gives them nothing to be suspicious about.

Sometimes Ruby barely gets back from Russia or somewhere before her parents come in to kiss her good night.

Sometimes she does this trick of stuffing pillows under the blanket so it looks like she's actually asleep when really she's fifteen-and-a-bit thousand miles away and not wearing her pajamas at all but probably instead a furry jacket, up a steep mountain.

I tell Betty, "I tried doing the pillows down the bed and it doesn't work, not if your mom is like mine and checks to see if you have brushed your teeth."

I say, "I don't think even Ruby Redfort could trick my mom."

Betty says, "What Ruby Redfort would do is to simply spray the smell of toothpaste in her room so her mother would smell the minty freshness and would just think she must have brushed her teeth and so wouldn't bother to check."

Of course, it's so simple! When you think about it.

The other equipment you simply must have if you are going to be a secretive agent is a telephone.

Ruby Redfort has telephones all over the place—even in the bathroom. Sometimes Hitch the butler carries them around on a tray.

Betty Moody's got one in her room.

I asked Dad if I could get a telephone in my room.

He laughed in a funny way for about almost nine minutes.

That's the thing about Betty's parents—they are really nice. Mr. and Mrs. Moody always say, "Call me Cecil" and "Call me Mol," and even Betty calls them Cecil and Mol.

They let Betty do whatever she wants, really, and she goes to bed whenever she likes.

Betty Moody is an only child.

Well, an almostly only child. She has a brother named Zack who is over twenty years old. He lives in an apartment and has a girlfriend who is from Japan.

I have an oldish brother called Kurt. Not many people get to see Kurt because he is usually in his room being alone. His room is full of gloom and a strange unpleasant smell. He keeps everything on the floor and no tidying is ever allowed.

Mom says, "It is all part of being a teenager and he will grow out of it one day."

I say, "When?"

Dad says, "Don't hold your breath."

Which means it could take a while.

Chapter 2

It is Monday, and the Ruby book I am reading right now at this exact instant is called RUBY REDFORT RULES. All the books start off the same way:

On a street called Cedarwood Drive was an ultra-modern house, white and gleaming with glass. And in that house lived a most unusual little girl, daughter to Brant and Sabina Redfort, socialites.

Brant and Sabina called their little girl Ruby, but to those in the know she was Ruby Redfort — secret agent, undercover detective, and mystery solver.

There is a picture of her house and a map of the secret getaway tunnels.

The books always start off really calm and cozy so you just don't know what you are in for.

It was a wonderful morning. Mrs. Digby drew back the curtains and the sun splashed on Ruby Redfort's angelic face.

"Muffins or French toast?" inquired the ever-thoughtful housekeeper.

"Muffins," yawned Ruby, stuffing her feet into remarkably fluffy slippers.

"Coming right up, Miss Ruby. I'll just go run you a bath. Take your time—no need to hurry."

You see, you can't help thinking it's going to be utterly boring. But just you wait.

Ruby could tell it was going to be a fabulous day. She just had a good feeling about —

"Mom says

you better get out of bed

right now,

and if you want milk on your Sugar Puffs,

too bad,

there isn't any."

That's my sister, Marcie—you can tell by the rudeness.

Mom says when manners were being handed out, Marcie must have been in the bathroom.

I have to

hop

down*stairs*

because I only have one slipper. Our dog, Cement, buried the other one in the yard and we can't find it.

It will probably be discovered in a hundred years from now by archaeological diggers who will say it is fascinating and give it to a museum.

When I get downstairs, the whole
kitchen is full of a bad mood.
Marcie won't talk to Mom, and
Kurt won't talk to Marcie.
Grandad isn't talking to anyone
because he hasn't plugged himself
into his hearing aid.
Minal is talking to me
but I wish he wouldn't.
Minal is a niggling gnat
and I have to have him sleeping in my room.
Sometimes, when I want to keep him out,
I pile lots of junk against the door.
He is five.

Who wants to share a room with
a five-year-old brother? I don't
even need a five-year-old brother.
I already have one who is a
teenager called Kurt and
that is enough brothers
for anyone.

Minal is going, "What time did the spider go to the dentist?"

I don't bother to listen to the answer because it won't be funny.

I am trying to read the back of the cereal box because there is a good offer for rubber pencil-tops.

Minal is going, "Spider clock!

D'ya get it? D'ya get it? Spider clock!"

I say, "No."

He is joggling me, which makes me spill my orange juice down my sweater.

So I give him a Chinese burn.

Mom says, "Clarice, you are really behaving like an earwig! Get your coat on and zip off to school quick-smart, no funny business. And pull your socks up, don't forget your packed lunch, and by the way, you've dribbled down your front."

Sometimes, if I can, I read my book walking to school.

Ruby took the elevator down from the kitchen to the front door.

"See you, Hitch," she called to the butler as she stepped inside the sleek black limo that was waiting outside. Ruby flicked on the onboard TV—she liked to tune into her favorite cartoons before the school day began. She enjoyed the ride; it was so hassle free —

"Clarice Beean, **Clarice Beean!** **Wait for me.** I'm right **behind you!"**

It's the boy from over the wall, Robert Granger. I try to ignore him and keep on reading my book.

"On second thought," said Ruby to her chauffeur, "I'll walk."

After all, it was a fabulous day and this way she could stop in at the mini-market and pick up some of that bubble gum she liked.

"Clarice Beean, I know you can hear me!"

Robert Granger!

He drives me just about loopy.

Sometimes he sits on the wall waiting for me to pop my head out of the door.

I spend half my time trying to get rid of him.

Mom says I am lucky and that I should take it as a compliment.

She says not everyone has someone who wants to be with them so much that they follow them around all day.

I say she is welcome to him. She can have him skipping behind her in his rain boots—see how lucky she feels.

Ruby Redfort has an annoying neighbor too, but he's seventyish and so isn't in her school class or anything but he is always poking his nose into other people's businesses, so in that way he is very similar to Robert Granger.

Mr. Parker stuck his nose out of his front door and sniffed very loudly.

"Is that that Redfort child? I've told you before, keep off my grass! Do your parents know where you are? Shouldn't you be in school? I've got a good mind to call them myself."

Ruby Redfort just acted like she couldn't hear a thing.

"Good morning, Mr. Parker," called Ruby cheerily. "How are you today?"

This always made Mr. Parker madder than ever.

I rush into school and Betty Moody is there already and she is wearing some strange fancy shoes that are foreign.

Betty Moody travels the world with her mom and dad and they have friends all over the planet, even in China, which is a gersquillion inches and miles from here at the very least.

Betty's parents say it is essential for a child to see the world if they are to become a well-rounded individual.

They say traveling the world is the best education a child could have, and they often fly Betty off somewhere at utterly just a moment's notice.

It's most unusual.

I wish Robert Granger would go off around the world.

He comes marching up to me and Betty and says, "Have you thought of your book exhibit idea yet because you should because there is going to be a mystery prize for the best book exhibit and you will get your name written on a little silver cup that goes on the glass trophy shelf and everyone will see it, it says so on the board, and me and Arnie Singh have thought of a really good exhibit and we are going to win."

Which of course is utterly unlikely, knowing them.

It turns out Robert Granger and Arnie Singh are doing an exhibit on dinosaurs.

They say they have got an original dinosaur's

prehistoric bones, but I know they are chicken bones from Robert's Sunday dinner.

I say, "Those bones are too small to be dinosaur bones."

And they say, "They are from a very tiny dinosaur."

I say, "There weren't any tiny dinosaurs. That is a chicken."

They say, "It is a chicken dinosaur."

I say, "That's interesting. I didn't know you could buy dinosaurs in the supermarket."

Mind you, it's got our minds whirring.

We look at the tiny winners' cup on the glass trophy shelf.

We really want to win it, and of course our heads are blank with no ideas.

Also, we are wondering what the mystery prize could be.

I think it might be a walkie-talkie and Betty thinks it will be one of those

Winner

cameras that gives you the pictures right away.
Whatever it is,
we want it.

After school, I go over to Betty Moody's house,
so we can talk about our exhibit.

I love going over to the Moodys'. It's really fun,
and sometimes supper is just pretzels and
a fizzy drink!

Usually though, Mr. Moody-Call-Me-Cecil says,
"Let's go out to the
Wah Chung."
Which is a Chinese
restaurant. It's
very smart,
with chairs of
purpley velvet.

Other times he
makes dinner out
of whatever
is in the cupboard—

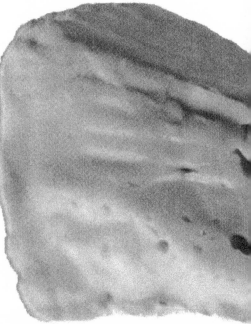

maybe just a potato and a strange-smelling cheese.

The Moodys live in a house that's modern, just like Ruby Redfort does.

You have to go upstairs to the kitchen.

It's
amazing.

When you go in, it's right away "Shoes off and special slippers on."

They learned that in Japan.

I have told Mom about it.

She says, "Clarice Bean! The times I have asked you to please take your shoes off and will you? No!"

It's true, but it's funny because at the Moodys' house it feels like fun.

We end up hardly talking about the book competition at all because we can't stop talking about Ruby Redfort.

Me and Betty are crazily reading the whole series.

We can't stop. And when we've finished, we'll read them over again.

I have just got to this bit where Ruby Redfort is running for class president and they are having a school election to vote for who is best.

Naturally, Mrs. Drisco, Ruby's teacher, is not pleased about this because Ruby and Mrs. Drisco do not see eye to eye. And of course Ruby has lots of good ideas for changing things, like e.g. making recess longer.

I just wish there were more Ruby books. I am thinking of writing to Patricia F. Maplin Stacey, who is the author, and telling her that she should write a bit more quickly.

Mrs. Moody-Call-Me-Mol says, "Why don't you? People always love to hear how much other people enjoy their books."

Betty's mom knows about this because she is in fact a writer.

She is going off to sign books abroad in another country on Wednesday.

She is utterly well known and you can buy her books in all the good bookstores.

So
we
write:

Dear Patricia F. Maplin Stacey,

We are avidish readers of the Ruby Redfort series
and we have read all of them at least once.
What we would like to know is when is the next Ruby
Redfort book coming out and what will it be called?

Also, on page a hundred and 6, chapter eight of
Run For It, Ruby

why did the arch villain Hogtrotter not double-check that he had locked the cellar door?

And also, on page 33 you said Ruby was wearing her glasses and then later on you say she couldn't see well because she didn't have her reading glasses.

Eagerly awaiting your reply,

Betty P. Moody and Clarice Bean Tuesday

p.S. We think you should write a bit faster.

We write two letters, one from each of us, in case one gets lost in the mail. Mol gives us stamps so we can mail them tomorrow.

She asks us what we are up to at school and we tell her about the boring book competition, which we want to win.

And she says, "Why do you have to pick a boring book?"

And she's right—why do we?

Except that we can't find one that is interesting and is also about learning.

Chapter 3

On Tuesday, I am a bit anxious because me and Betty Moody still haven't thought of a book project.

Also, I am late because I can't stop reading RUBY REDFORT RULES.

Ruby sauntered into school, not bothering to hurry. After all, she was already twenty minutes late. What difference would another five make? She could always come up with an excuse. She had to get past Mrs. Bexenheath, the school secretary, but that wasn't hard.

Mrs. Bexenheath was no match for Ruby's excuses. No matter how hard the poor secretary tried, she just couldn't get Ruby to admit she was up to something.

It was Mrs. Drisco who was the problem. No one was as strict as Mrs. Drisco. Mrs. Drisco made the evil Count von Viscount seem like a pussycat.

Ruby swaggered into the classroom and slumped down at her desk, lolling back in her chair. But to Ruby Redfort's enormous surprise, a telling-off did not follow, and instead Mrs. Drisco beamed a friendly smile at her.

Mrs. Drisco was being nice! Now, that didn't seem right.

And as the lesson wore on, Ruby realized that she wasn't bored! It was unthinkable to find

Mrs. Drisco's lessons anything but boring.

Something was definitely a bit fishy.

Had Mrs. Drisco been turned into some kind of a Martian? Or had she been replaced by an impostor Mrs. Drisco?

Too bad Mrs. Wilberton hasn't been turned into a Martian. First of all, she gives me a mean look for lateness, and then she says, "I hope everybody has had a good think about what their book project will be. Anyone who hasn't chosen a book will be given one by me."

These words give me the shivers

because I know the kind of book Mrs. Wilberton would pick. Probably something like the secret life of a snail, or ballet, or snails that do ballet.

Betty and me look at each other and I make a face that means, "Help—what shall we do?"

And she makes a face that means, "How should I know?"

I am beginning to panic because if we can't think of anything, then we will be in trouble and we will get a telling-off and then we will have to do one of Mrs. Wilberton's dreary ideas.

Why hasn't Betty Moody come up with a good plan?

She is good at thinking of things that will keep Mrs. Wilberton happy.

She utterly never gets in trouble.

It's true!

Never!

It's as if Betty has been zapped by the dastardly Count von Viscount.

It's like that bit in WHO WILL RESCUE RUBY REDFORT?

when Count von Viscount tries to brainwash Ruby and steal all her good ideas.

He does it by making his eyes go goggly, and before you know it, you are under his spell.

Mrs. Wilberton is going around the class—she is almost at me.

Alexandra Holker says she is doing her exhibit on the olden-day times because she loves the past.

She says she is going to dress up in an ancient outfit and pretend she is from a hundred years ago and give out Victorian fudges. She got the idea from a book called The Victorians.

I have to admit, I wish I had thought of that.

And my cousin Noah and my friend Suzie Woo say they are doing their project on a book called Global Grub, which is about food from around the world, and they are going to have actual real-life food in their exhibit.

Mrs. Wilberton is almost about to say my name and I can feel my stomach niggling with nerves, but just as she says, "Clarice Bean, what is your book competition entry?" Mrs. Marse pops her head around the door and says, "Mrs. Wilberton, Mr. Pickering would like a word."

And then, just like that,

she beetles off.

After recess, Mrs. Wilberton is huffing and puffing about something or other.

It's probably Karl Wrenbury's fault.

It usually is.

Karl Wrenbury is the naughtiest boy in my school and he is in my class.

He gets in trouble at least once a day.

One time he got into the janitor's closet and stole some signs that said

THIS TOILET IS OUT OF ORDER!

He stuck them on all the doors, including Mr. Pickering's office.

He got sent home for that.

Mrs. Marse says he is probably hyperactive and

that he should be kept off the sugary drinks.

Mrs. Wilberton says there is no excuse for bad behavior and that Karl Wrenbury is just determined to be a disruptive influence and spoil it for the others.

I overheard her talking to Mr. Skippard, the janitor. She said, "I blame the parents."

And Mr. Skippard said, "I couldn't agree more."

Mrs. Wilberton says, "I am disappointed to tell you that somebody, naming no names, you know who you are, has been messing around before school and has flooded the boys' toilets."

I am a bit fidgety in case it is me, although I haven't even been in the boys' toilets, ever.

It turns out it is Karl Wrenbury and also Toby Hawkling.

They have to go and see Mr. Pickering and they don't come back.

When it's time to go home, I go to my peg to put my coat on, but something funny has happened to the sleeves and it has a zipper instead of buttons. The exactly same thing has happened to the other coats.

It turns out all the coats have managed to get on the wrong pegs. It takes ages to find mine.

I wonder how it happened—Karl Wrenbury wasn't even at school this afternoon.

Spooky.

On the way back to my house, I have to stop off to buy some essentials, which is mainly potato chips. Unfortunately when I come out of the shop, Robert Granger is standing outside.

I utterly don't want to walk
home with him so I have to
go the long way around.
As soon as I get in the front
door, I start to notice that
things are strange and
something is a bit odd in
the living room.
Then I
realize — the
television is
not on and
Grandad is not in
his chair.
The other thing,
which is a bit slightly
odd, is I can hear a
strange yelping noise, or
is it yapping?
I am not sure where
it is coming from.

It's not from Cement anyway, because he is standing next to me, eating the message pad.

I try and wrestle it from him because I can see that he is about to swallow a message from someone but I don't know who.

The only words I can read say, "didn't have time to tell you, but going to Rus . . ."

What can it mean?

Who didn't have time to tell who? And why are they in a rush?

I am just wondering what to do when the telephone rings.

It's Mom. She says, "Clarice, could you tell your brother to put dinner in the oven?"

I say, "There's something fishy happening. I can hear someone yapping—"

She says, "Mrs. Pargett! Not like that. You'll do yourself a mischief. I'm coming! Don't move! Wait there!"

And then the line goes dead.

Mom works at the old people's center and is teaching them dancing.

She says dancing can be very dangerous if your hips aren't what they once were.

Anyway, I get my little notebook out and I write down:

Very strange occurrence in the living room.

That's the kind of thing Ruby Redfort would say.

Missing Grandad
and a yelping or is it a yapping noise?
Mom doesn't seem bothered.

What is going on?

I underline that several times because

that is the

big
question.

Kurt shrivels dinner, and it tastes burned but that isn't odd.

What's spooking me is that he seems happy!

I will tell Betty Moody about it tomorrow.

Chapter 4

On Wednesday, as soon as I get up, I start reading again. I even read walking downstairs to breakfast.

> Ruby Redfort sauntered into the kitchen, where the wonderful Mrs. Digby was already preparing pancakes.
>
> They smelled unbelievably mouth-watering.

Dad says, "What would you like for breakfast?"

I say, "Pancakes."

Dad says, "If you want pancakes, you can make them yourself."

I say, "All right, then, I will."

Mom says, "We've run out of eggs."

Mrs. Digby would never run out of eggs.

When I get to school, Betty Moody is nowhere to be seen.

I wonder what has happened. She is utterly, absolutely never not ever late for class. Except very rarely.

Maybe she has got the chicken pox or an infectious temperature.

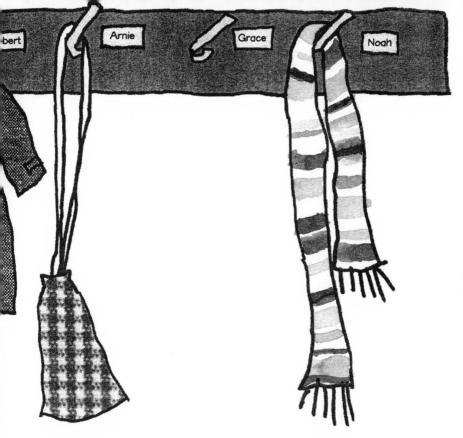

Grace Grapello isn't here either, hoorah!

The worst thing is there is no escaping telling Mrs. Wilberton what our project is going to be.

I am thinking, *What would Ruby Redfort do in this situation?*

Ruby Redfort can always think of a snappy answer when Mrs. Drisco is on her tail.

She would say something like: "Well, Mrs. Drisco, the thing is, I was walking along, minding my own business, when, what do you know, but I got pounced on by this whole group of wild cats and, in my desperate attempt to fight them off, I hit my head and am now suffering from amnesia."

Which is forgetting your memory.

"And so you see, Mrs. Drisco, I am unable to tell you about my book exhibit, on account of the fact that it has been wiped from my mind, and if you don't believe me, just call our butler, Hitch."

And then Mrs. Drisco might say, "Well, Miss Redfort, I think I might just do that."

And of course, when she calls Hitch, he says, "Oh yes, Mrs. Drisco, I am afraid that's exactly what happened."

Hitch always backs Ruby up.

I wish I had a butler, but Dad says butlers are very expensive.

"Clarice Bean! For the third and final time, would you please answer my question!"

And before I can stop myself I say, "Umm, wh-what was the question, Mrs. Drisco?"

Mrs. Wilberton looks at me with scrunkled eyes and says, "Well, missy, it may be too much for you to remember, but everyone else here knows that my name is Mrs.

W.I.L.B.E.R.T.O.N.

That's Wilberton."

Mrs. Wilberton says, "The question was, what is your book exhibit going to be about and are you going to enter the competition?"

I am looking down at my desk, staring at my book, RUBY REDFORT RULES, and I am just about to tell Mrs. Wilberton the amnesia excuse when something accidentally pops out of my mouth. I don't really mean to say it, but it's a bit like Ruby Redfort often says, "Sometimes the answer is right under your nose. And sometimes you just have to come up with an answer even if it is maybe sort of the wrong answer."

What I say is, "Yes, Mrs. Wilberton, me and Betty Moody will be doing an exhibit on Ruby Redfort, secret agent and arch detective."

Everyone is in a stunned silence because they wish they'd thought of it.

Mrs. Wilberton is in a stunned silence because she doesn't think it is such a good idea.

I know this because she makes her mouth go all tight and then says, "I do not think this is such a good idea."

She says, "Just what do you imagine you have learned from these books?"

And of course, that's the catch. I can't think of anything I have learned from them, but I am sure Betty will think of something.

I walk home in an utterly
excited mood.

Ruby Redfort was thrilled! She had got the better of that Mrs. Drisco. Well, this time, anyway.

Mrs. Drisco was determined to thwart Ruby's attempts to be class president and stop her from making the changes to school uniforms and recess that everybody was crying out for.

When I get home, I call Betty to tell her the good news, but no one is picking up the receiver.

I am beginning to get worried.

Maybe all the Moodys are ill in bed with the chicken pox.

But even if they were, they would still be able to answer the telephone because they have telephones in their bedrooms in case of emergencies like the chicken pox.

I can hear that yapping again, and it's coming from Grandad's room, and there is no doubt that it is not Cement because Cement does not yap.

Also, Grandad is out giving him his walk—he has left a note.

I look through the keyhole and I think I can see something moving and it can't be our cat, Fuzzy, because he is standing next to me.

Something is peculiar.

I decide to have a quick peek in his room, but just then I hear Grandad opening the front door, and so I quickly pick up the telephone and pretend to be talking to Mrs. Stampney, our neighbor.

This is exactly the kind of thing that Ruby Redfort would do.

The only problem is, Grandad hears me pretending to be chatting to Mrs. Stampney, who, P.S. I do not like one iota, and then Grandad asks me to ask Mrs. Stampney if he can borrow her spare

dog basket for some strange reason.

Now that means I will have to specially
call Mrs. Stampney—otherwise
he will smell
a rat.

That never happens to Ruby Redfort.

Then Grandad says, "By the way, your friend
Betty called this morning."

I eagerly say, "Did she leave a message?"

And he says, "She said something about rushing.
I didn't hear what else she was talking about
because the line was crackly."

Rushing? Why was Betty Moody rushing?

Was something chasing her?

After supper, I'm eager to get back to my book.

I can't read in Mom's closet because, mysteriously, my flashlight has gone missing and may well be stolen.

Instead I have to read in my room.

At the moment, I am reading this bit—it's very exciting—I am literally on the edge of my wits.

> Night fell like a cloak over the city. There wasn't a single star twinkling. It was as if there was no sky at all.

You see, already it's gripping.

> Ruby Redfort was lying on her bed, eating pizza and drinking cola. She hadn't changed out of her school uniform and was still wearing her clunky school shoes.

My mom would go utterly crazy if I lay on my bed with my shoes on.

Playing on the super-deluxe wrap-around sound TV was Ruby Redfort's favorite show, CRAZY COPS, starring Dirk Draylon, possibly the most handsome man on the planet.

There was a polite knock at the door.

"Enter," called Ruby, her mouth crammed full of pizza.

The door swung open and in glided her trusty friend and butler, Hitch.

On a silver tray was a pink and shiny telephone. It was just one of Ruby Redfort's many telephones.

"A Mr. Hogtrotter for you, Miss Redfort. He's most insistent that he speak to you."

Ruby sat up suddenly. The glass of cola fell to the floor.

She plucked up the receiver and, cool as a cucumber, said, "It's been a long time, Porky. I thought perhaps you'd retired."

"Not me, Miss Goody-Goody," replied the high, squeaky yet somehow sinister voice.

"So whaddya want this time? I really don't feel like a chat. I got a pizza getting cold here."

"Don't worry, I won't keep you. I just thought you might be interested to know that Dirk Draylon might not be getting so much airtime these days on account of he's working for a friend of mine . . . someone you ain't so keen on."

And with that the line went dead.

It couldn't be! thought Ruby. Not—She couldn't bring herself to even think his name. Surely Dirk Draylon would never work for . . . it was unimaginable! Impossible! Out of the question!

Ruby replaced the handset and said, "Hitch, I'll be needing my scuba gear."

I get up to switch out the light and guess what? Grandad is tiptoeing across the yard in his slippers! He's got my flashlight—the rapscallion! When he gets to the toolshed, he opens the door and goes inside. Is he losing his mind???

Or is he

up to something?

Whatever he is doing, it is something most definitely strange, and I am determined to get to the bottom of it, if it's the last thing I do. I have to go and switch the light on again so I can write that down in my little notebook. I wish I had one of those tiny tape recorders like Ruby Redfort has—it makes things much easier and you don't have to keep getting up and down to turn the light on and off.

Chapter 5

On Thursday, I have swimming club.

I don't really like going—it's a bit cold.

I just go because you get snacks afterward.

I'm not a strong swimmer—
I can't dive for a brick in pajamas or anything.
Betty Moody can.

But I'm not sure why you need to learn to rescue
a brick while you are wearing pajamas because
you will hardly ever find yourself wearing pajamas
when you have to rescue something.

It's a very rare emergency.

Betty Moody has goggles and everything and she
might become Olympic—she's got a badge.
Robert Granger can only do the doggy-paddle.
He is a splasher, and sometimes he swims with his
feet walking along the bottom.

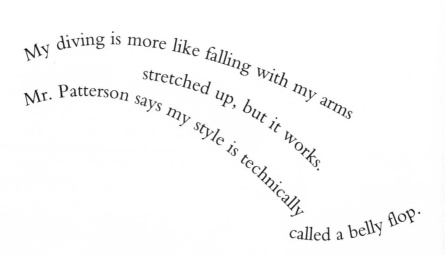

My diving is more like falling with my arms
stretched up, but it works.
Mr. Patterson says my style is technically
called a belly flop.

Mr. Patterson is a bit down in the mouth because

Betty Moody is missing swimming practice, and she is our team hopeful.

I am a bit down in the mouth because I am missing Betty Moody.

I have
no idea
where she is.

The only interesting thing that happened today was that Karl Wrenbury was chasing Toby Hawkling around the pool, trying to pull his trunks down as a joke.

But then he fell in the deep end and started drowning slightly, and Mr. Patterson

    had to quickly

                fling

              off

              his

              sneakers

                and dive in, in shorts!

And he said,

"That's why there is a rule that says

          no monkeying around

            the swimming pool!"

And,

"Next time, Karl Wrenbury

           might not be so lucky,

     and he will be a goner."

It was very dramatic, and when I get home,
I draw a picture of Karl Wrenbury nearly
drowning and send it to my granny—she likes
to hear the news.

Before bed, I have several tries at getting into
the bathroom so I can brush my teeth.

But mysteriously there is always someone
in there.

I decide to wait outside the door, reading
my book.

Ruby plopped backward off the speedboat and
dived down under the calm velvety black water.

She swam effortlessly. Only the bubbles from
her breathing confirmed that she was human
rather than fish.

Finally she saw it. The faint glimmer of
a light . . . a window.

As she approached, a circular entranceway
slid open. Ruby glided in.

Once inside, she climbed a ladder up out of the water and into a brilliant white chamber, where she changed out of her wetsuit and into dry clothes.

She was greeted by a voice on the intercom.

"Good evening, Ruby. Always a pleasure to see you, but I take it this isn't just a social call."

"No. You could say I need some help. Things have been getting pretty weird in Twinford lately and I can't help feeling it might all lead back to you-know-who."

There was a pause.

"Are you sure?"

"Well, not sure, exactly—it's more of a hunch, but it has his handiwork written all over it. You know, people behaving strangely, things not quite how they oughta be. I don't know. I've just got a funny feeling that something big's gonna happen, and you know how I am with funny feelings."

"Yes," came the voice, "you're usually right."

I wait really quite a long while, until finally the bathroom door is opened.

And guess who comes out?

Kurt.

Being in a bathroom is not at all normal for him.

My mom says Kurt can be a bit of a stranger to hygiene. To get hygiene, you must use soap and water.

He is smelling of clean and not even a bit like toadstools.

Chapter 6

On Friday, in the morning, things are even more fishy, and I am beginning to smell a rat.

For starters, I can't find my hairbrush.

It is missing.

Mom is being a bit

weirdishly behaved. She lets me eat my cereal in front of the TV, which is normally a NO-NO due to possible spillages, and milk is a devil to get out of upholstery.

I am pleased because it is Dippy Dog and His Pal, Dribble. It's an absolutely funny cartoon about a stupid dog and his friend, a rat that dribbles.

I wish I had thought of that idea.

Imagine thinking of that.

The TV people think of so many good ideas. That's what they must do all day—think and think.

Imagine being paid to think.

I would love to be in the TV business.

I've got loads of ideas.

I am nonstop thinking of things.

I could probably earn squillions a week
for my thinking.

Then the phone rings and I overhear Mom going,
"Yes? Oh really? Oh no, what? Oh dear heavens,
I'll be right over."

Then Mom shouts, "Clarice, Minal, quick, get
in the car or you will be late for school!"

I say, "But Mom, it's only seven-thirty!"

She says, "Well imagine how surprised Mrs.
Wilberton will be when you arrive early."

And I say, "Imagine how surprised Mrs.
Wilberton will be when I arrive in my pajamas."

And she says, "Well, you've got precisely five
seconds to find something resembling
a school uniform!"

I say, "What the dickens is going on?"

And she says, "I haven't got time to explain.
Now, move it!"

I mean that was odd, wasn't it?

I arrive at school at 7:45 A.M.

No one is there except the cleaner, who gives me a cookie from the janitor's closet.

I ask her about the mysterious incident with the coats swapping themselves, and she says that Mr. Skippard had to move them all when the boys' toilets got flooded.

She said everything was in a terrible state so Mr. Skippard decided to give the whole place a really good spring clean.

She says, "Mr. Skippard even cleaned the shelf that holds all the school trophy cups and everything."

She says, "You name it, it's been cleaned."

I was slightly hoping for it to be more mysterious than that, but I suppose it's good to have something solved.

When Mrs. Wilberton sees me, she says a rude comment about me actually being on time for once and that it's a shame I couldn't manage to really make her day and brush my hair.

She says, "Clarice Bean, you look like you've been dragged through a hedge backward."

I wish someone would drag Mrs. Wilberton through a hedge backward.

She is as bad as that Mrs. Drisco and I wouldn't be surprised if Patricia F. Maplin Stacey didn't get the idea for Mrs. Drisco from meeting Mrs. Wilberton.

In class, some people are talking about their exhibits.

I am trying not to talk about mine because I am trying to keep it as top-secret as possible because there might be copying from you-know-who, plus other people I could mention.

If only Betty Moody was here, I could talk top-secretly to her.

But she is not in school again.

No one knows where she is.

Grace Grapello hasn't heard my idea yet because she was luckily away when I came up with it.

I know what Bridget Garnett is doing—just the sort of project Mrs. Wilberton would like.

She has chosen a book called *The Wonderful World Down Under*, about Australia.

Her exhibit is going to be kangaroos and their habits.

She says she is going to spend the whole day hopping, just to see what it feels like.

Andrew Hickley is doing the same, but with wallabies.

After lunch, I am getting even more fed up with Mrs. Wilberton than usual.

She says my spelling is a bit here and there, and it's interesting how I can spell the same word so many different ways.

She says, "Keep guessing and the probability is one day you will be right."

I wish I had my old teacher, Mrs. Nesbit. She was really nice and she would say "Well done" just for even slightly trying.

Nowadays trying your hardest just isn't enough for some people I could mention beginning with W.

Dad always says I should just try and stay out of her way.

What I want to know is HOW, when I am in her class every single day?

I wish I was grown up.

Dad says, "It doesn't get any easier. You still have someone bossing you around."

He says he finds Mr. Thorncliff, his boss, very tricky and he tries to steer clear of him as much as possible.

I say, "At least you get paid to be bossed around. I get bossed around for free."

I can't concentrate because I am busy imagining Mrs. Wilberton as a hippopotamus, and I am writing:

Mrs. Wilberton is a hippipotimis.

Mrs. Wilberton is a hippipotimis.

over and over again, without really meaning to. And what I am unaware of is that Mrs. Wilberton is standing behind me, reading it.

She says, "Can anyone here correctly spell the word *hippopotamus* for Clarice Bean?"

Of course, Robert Granger puts his hand up, which is a joke because he is the last person who would be able to spell hippopotamus.

Luckily for me, Mrs. Marse comes trotting in.

Mrs. Marse looks a little bit like a hedgehog in high heels.

She says, "Can Clarice Bean please come to the secretary's office, where there is a waiting mother?"

Everyone looks at me leaving because they
know I must have something really important
going on since I am going to miss half of an
afternoon of Mrs. Wilberton being dreary.

Mom is walking very fast across the playground,
and I have to almost run to keep up.

When I get into
the car, Minal is
there chatting
to himself like a
twit.

Mom says,
"Sorry to drag
you out of class
early but you
would not
believe the
morning
I have had!
There will

be no one at home to let you in after school so you are just going to have to come with me."

She says, "If it's not one thing, it's a-blimming-nother."

I say, "Where is Grandad? Why isn't he at home?"

Mom says, "Grandad has got himself into some very hot water."

It turns out that he has been banned from visiting his best friend, Bert-the-Shirt Finch, at the Evergreens Old People's Home.

And that Bert-the-Shirt Finch might be actually asked to please move out of Evergreens since he obviously cannot behave like a responsible senior citizen and abide by other people's rules.

Until the week before last, he lived in his own apartment with a Pekingese and a German shepherd, but the people in the know said he wasn't managing the stairs so well and what with one thing and another he had to be moved into an aged persons' home with round-the-clock supervision.

It was for his

own good.

Bert said he didn't mind moving and that it would be nice to get his meals cooked for him. Since the only thing he was eating before was cheese on toast and sometimes just cheese on nothing.

But the slightly big problem is Evergreens Old Folks' Home is strictly no dogs allowed and absolutely no cats, either.

You may have a parakeet.

Mom says, "Everyone thought Bert had given his dogs to Mrs. Cartwell."

But, oh no, a certain person called Grandad has

been keeping Flossie, the German shepherd, in our toolshed and the Pekingese, Ralph, in his actual room, and every night he has been smuggling them secretly into Bert's bedroom at the Evergreens. And every morning he collects them and brings them home.

Unfortunately, Ralph escaped and chewed Mrs. Perkins's parakeet, Oliver, until he was actually dead.

And Mrs. Perkins has lodged a complaint against Grandad and Bert, and Mom is left to pick up the pieces.

We have to wait in the corridor while Mom sorts things out for Bert and tries to get him in somewhere else where you can have a pet. Which is easier said than done.

Bert doesn't have a family, except for a long-lost son in Alaska, and Mom says someone's got to come to the rescue.

Minal manages to spend one hour

pretending to drive a toilet-roll car around the carpet. Thank goodness I have my book.

Ruby Redfort arrived back home after a long, hard day at school. She kicked off her shoes and ran upstairs to the kitchen.

Mrs. Redfort was there, busying herself with whatever it was Mrs. Redfort did, and Mr. Redfort was reading the sports section.

Hitch was preparing elaborate fruit cocktails. Catching Ruby's eye, Hitch pointed discreetly at his watch. Ruby nodded.

Time was short—Hitch and Ruby were expected at headquarters at 1700 hours.

"Hi, Mom! Hi, Dad! I just gotta go look at some history—you know, homework."

"Of course, my darling. I'm glad you are paying so much attention to your studies. What are you learning about these days?" inquired her mother.

"You know, stuff," replied Ruby evasively.

Luckily the phone rang, and Sabina Redfort became engrossed in a conversation with Mrs. Irshman about arranging cut flowers.

"Quick, Ruby!" whispered Hitch. "We don't have much time. I need to get you to headquarters before —"

"Oh, Ruby, sweetheart . . ." called out her father, but Ruby was already halfway up to her room.

"See you later, Dad. Gotta study!"

"But Ruby!" continued her father. "Just to let you know, your mother and I would very much like it if you joined us for dinner this evening. Marjorie and Freddy are coming over with their son, Quent. Supper will be served at eight. Ooh and sweetheart, wear something nice."

"Darn," sighed Ruby under her breath.

Apart from the nightmare of making it back in time, Quent was a real yawn.

Mr. and Mrs. Redfort know nothing about Hitch's life as a secret agent helper. They have no idea that being a butler is just a sideline to him.

We get home and Kurt has cooked supper for us.

It's not too bad actually.

But I can't help noticing that he has been using a hairbrush on himself.

Kurt doesn't have a hairbrush!

I bet he's been using mine, the weasel.

I am so busy thinking about this that I almost don't notice the letter on the table, which is addressed to me, with my name on it.

I open it right away.

Inside is a postcard of Patricia F. Maplin Stacey in a pantsuit. It's the same picture as the one on the back of every single Ruby Redfort book.

The letter says:

Dear Betty and Clarace

Thank you for your kind inquiry.
In answer to your question,
the next Ruby book will be
published this fall.
The title is yet to be announced.

Patricia F. Maplin Stacey hopes you
continue to enjoy her books and
wishes you happy reading!

Yours truly,

Patricia F. Maplin Stacey

Creator of the Ruby Redfort Collection

Details of the fan club are listed
on the Ruby Redfort website.

I was hoping to get a slightly more helpful letter—it is not what I was expecting, and I don't think Patricia F. Maplin Stacey even wrote the letter herself.

It looked a bit typed and my name was spelled wrong and I am sure Patricia F. Maplin Stacey is a good speller.

When Dad hears all about Mom's dreadful day, he says, "It sounds like Grandad really is in the doghouse."

Mom says, "Right now, I do not find that remark one bit funny."

Chapter 7

I have the whole Weekend to worry and wonder about what has happened to Betty Moody. And the first thing I do is wake up at seven o'clock on Saturday with my mind already thinking the worst.

One thought I had was that Mol and Cecil had sent Betty to boarding school, because I have read about that happening to people in books when the parents get fed up with them. But Cecil and Mol never get fed up with Betty—they utterly take her everywhere.

Also, Cecil and Mol have disappeared too, and no one is answering the phone, not even the answering machine itself.

Maybe the Moodys are on the run from the law, or maybe Cecil has invented an invention and someone wickedish is trying to steal it and the Moodys have had to go into hiding.

Like in the book RUN FOR IT, RUBY.

Or maybe they have all been captured, and if they don't hand over the secret formula, they will be dropped into a bubbling volcano, which is what happened to Ruby Redfort in WHERE IN THE WORLD ARE YOU, RUBY REDFORT?

In the story, it's up to Ruby's best friend, Clancy Crew, to solve the puzzle of the missing Ruby and follow all these clues. Clancy Crew is quite often having to do this.

Even in this book RUBY REDFORT RULES, I have got to this bit where Ruby seems to have disappeared, but don't worry, it's all part of her secret agent work.

Clancy Crew tried to remember all the things Ruby had said during their telephone conversation just the other night. That had been the last time Clancy had heard from Ruby. Had Ruby been trying to tell him something?

Maybe she had been captured by some arch villain and was trying to let Clancy know her whereabouts in some sort of code. Now that Clancy thought of it, it did seem strange that Ruby had mentioned that she was having tapioca pudding in China. Ruby Redfort hated tapioca pudding—everybody knew that! And just what was she doing in China?

In the story, Clancy does some quick thinking and works out that tapioca stands for BAD NEWS (because tapioca is bad news if you don't like it), in just stands for IN, and China stands for City Help I Need Advice.

So the message is:

BAD NEWS. IN CITY. HELP! I NEED ADVICE.

It's so clever, I wish I knew code.

I get a sort of clue when I go downstairs. It's come in the mail.

It's a postcard with a picture of a strange curly-shaped building on it and the words

Wish you were here!

The corner is torn off and I can't read who it is from.

Of course, it could be from Betty because there is a *B* and it is written in Betty's handwriting.

Maybe she is probably trying to tell me something . . .

but what?

I run to show Mom, but she is busy chatting
to Kurt.

That may not seem odd to you but
if you know him, you know
Kurt never just chats.

Chapter 8

On
Sunday,
I go over
to my friend
Alexandra Holker's.
She is eating pizza
and she tells me what
happened at school after I
had to leave for the emergency.

What she says is that Toby Hawkling and Karl Wrenbury told Mrs. Wilberton they were doing the dictionary as their book exhibit. And Mrs. Wilberton said something like, "What an awfully good idea indeed."

And Toby Hawkling said, "We are going to write down lots of words and print them up really giantly and stick them in the corridor." Mrs. Wilberton said, "Well, for once, Karl Wrenbury and Toby Hawkling, I actually approve."

Unfortunately, she changed her mind when she saw the words they had chosen.

She said, "Well, if you two like words so much, I have got just the thing for you."

She kept them in all recess.

She made them write:

I am not smart. I am not clever.

over and over again, at least a hundred times.

She said, "They are not to be in a pair because

they can't conduct themselves like mature, grown-up children, and one of them is always egging the other one on and they just spend their valuable learning time being silly."

She said, "If they can't behave like decent little boys, then too bad, they won't be treated like decent little boys."

She said, "I won't have it! Do you hear me? I won't have it!"

Chapter 9

Until Monday, I thought it was quite funny, but today when Mrs. Wilberton says, "Since Betty has decided not to bother to come to school for the past few days, Clarice Bean can join up with Karl Wrenbury."

Of course, I am utterly speechless.

To make matters worse, when a certain person beginning with G named Grace Grapello finds out that I am allowed to do Ruby Redfort, she says that she is too and that it was her idea all along and it is me that is copying her. And that she is going to do a Ruby Redfort exhibit.

Mrs. Wilberton says, "Absolutely no way, José!" Then she says, "In fact I am not even sure anyone is going to be doing an exhibit based on such drivel."

Mrs. Wilberton starts being very critical of my idea. She says, "The Ruby Redfort series is not a good example of the literature of our times."

How can she say this?????

I say one of my ideas is to make badges because Ruby's got these great phrases that she says a lot and they would make good badges and people could wear them.

Things like:

and

Mrs. Wilberton says Ruby Redfort has got an unpleasant turn of phrase and is unsuitable material for little girls.

She says, "These books are encouraging girls to run wild and I would prefer it if you picked a new project — how about ballet dancing?"

She says, "If you will insist on doing this Redfort book, you will have to go and talk to Mr. Pickering. Maybe he can talk some sense into you."

Mr. Pickering says, "I think it is fine to do the Ruby books as your exhibit, because enjoying reading is important. I'm all for it.

"However, part of the book exhibit is about choosing a book that you have learned something from. And you can have a chance of winning the cup and the mystery prize only if you can tell everybody what that is."

Mr. Pickering says he is very much looking forward to seeing what I come up with.

He says he has bought the Ruby Redfort books for his niece and that he wishes he had time to read them himself—they sound very exciting.

And I say,

"They are."

I come out of Mr. Pickering's office and there is Grace Grapello, doing her sneering face and she says something like, "Copycat."

And I say,

"It is you that is copying me and you know it."

And she says, "Liar!"

And I say, "Big bum!"

Grace Grapello is my archenemy. The reason she is my worst person at school, apart from Mrs. Wilberton, is because she is such a know-it-all and she is always annoying me with annoying comments and she can be really a meanie.

Once she invited Betty Moody to her birthday skating party without asking me.

She isn't even a friend of Betty Moody's.

Betty said, "No, thank you, Grace. I am going to tea with my utterly best friend, Clarice Bean."

And that was that, and that is why Betty Moody is my absolutely best friend.

Mom says, "I am afraid you will always bump into girls like Grace Grapello. I remember at my school there was a nasty piece of work called Felicity Marchmont. She used to put chewing gum in my gym shoes and tell people I had fleas."

Mom says the only way to deal with girls like Felicity is to feel sorry for them. They must be very sad people if the only pleasure they get is making other people absolutely not like them.

I say, "I can't feel sorry for Grace Grapello because she is too

utterly horrible."

Mom says, "Fair enough, then just picture her as
a
slug."

When I get back to class, I have to think really hard about what is going to be the learning part of my exhibit.

I am sure there is lots of learning in the Ruby Redfort books.

There must be because they are about someone really clever and it is written by someone really clever.

So it means I must have learned something, but what?

During recess I read a bit more of RUBY REDFORT RULES to see if I can quickly learn something.

Ruby rounded the corner and ran straight into her archenemy, Vapona Begwell, who was hanging out by the water fountain, talking to her friend Gemma Melamare.

They were discussing the school election and who was going to be voted class president.

"Just so long as it isn't that Ruby Redfort kid, then, win or lose, I really couldn't care," sneered Vapona.

"Oh, you are going to win for sure, Vapona," replied Gemma, patting her friend on the back.

"Hey, Gem, can you smell a funny smell?" said the gravelly-voiced Vapona, pretending to sniff the air. "Oh, hi, Ruby—there you are."

"Hi, bugwart," replied Ruby. "Did you take a look in the mirror lately? You seem to have something weird on your face—oh no, my mistake, it's just your nose."

After school, Karl Wrenbury comes up to me and says he doesn't want to do

a **stupid** girls' book

about a **stupid girl,**

and that it will be really

stupid and boring.

I say, "Oh, really! So it is stupid to be an undercover secret agent and to rescue people using just your wits and some newfangled gadgets, is it?

"And I suppose fighting arch evildoers and flying about in a purplish helicopter is boring to someone like you who only comes to school on a little bike."

And I say, "For your information, they are going to make it into a Hollywood movie."

I can tell he's quite impressed.

And once I have told him about the slimeball Hogtrotter, arch rapscallion, and I have happened to mention about how the evil Count von Viscount tries to drop Ruby Redfort and Clancy

Crew into a bubbling volcano, but Hitch rescues them in exactly the nick of time, then he is suddenly quite intrigued.

He says he isn't so interested in the rescuing bit, but the rest of it is quite good.

I lend him WHERE IN THE WORLD ARE YOU, RUBY REDFORT? He has to promise not to let his dog chew it.

Then I show Karl the postcard of the curly buildings, which all clues point to being from Betty Moody, and he says she has probably been kidnapped by aliens who want to take over the world.

This is just the sort of thing I was afraid of.

So when I get home, I call Granny and she gets me to describe the picture.

She doesn't say anything for a couple of minutes and there is a strange choking sound.

And then Granny says, in a slightly strange, whispery voice, "I'm sorry, I've just swallowed a peppermint. I will have to call you back."

When she does, she says, "It sounds very much to me as if our friend Betty is in Russia."

Chapter 10

On Tuesday, Grace Grapello and Cindy Fisher say they are going to do the history of ballet. They have chosen a book called Dance Magic.

Mrs. Wilberton looks utterly pleased. This is exactly the type of book project that she would love. She says, "Well, girls, I very much look forward to seeing what you do because ballet is a personal passion of mine."

Grace Grapello looks at me with a slimy smile, which makes me want to be slightly sick.

Mrs. Wilberton tells Toby Hawkling he has to go in their group.

He does not look so pleased.

Later when I tell Granny, she says, "Grace Grapello is obviously completely desperate and will stop at nothing to win."

It's weird but Karl Wrenbury actually has some quite good ideas.

He says he is working on something at home, which he says means we will most likely win the competition and we will get the little cup with our names on which everyone will see, including Grace Grapello.

Toby Hawkling is being a nuisance and trying to put Karl off.

He says, "Ha ha ha, you are doing a girls' book."

And Karl says, "So what. You are doing ballet."

Toby Hawkling creeps back to his desk.

I invite Karl over after school, but he says he is up to his ears making a scene from Ruby Redfort.

But he will just come over for maybe an hour and a quarter.

He is dreadfully busy.

He's doing a model of the volcano where Count von Viscount is about to finish Ruby Redfort and

Clancy Crew off, and Count von Viscount says, "Farewell, you meddling kids!" and then he does this chilling laugh.

And Karl is going to do a recording of a chilling laugh and play it over and over on a tiny tape recorder.

He just needs to find a chilling laugh so he can tape it.

Not as easy as you might think.

He says he thinks Ruby Redfort isn't so bad, considering it's just a girls' book.

I say, "Ruby Redfort is not just a girls' book. It's an everyone book. Mr. Pickering himself is going to read them."

Later, at my house, Karl Wrenbury is actually being quite incredibly funny.

He can make his eyes go in different directions both at the same time.

He says he will teach my brother Minal how to do it if he wants.

And he can drink orange juice through a straw up his nose.

When I tell Mom, she says this is extraordinary but not necessarily something to do at the dinner table.

I say, "But you should see it—it is utterly amazing."

Mom says she enjoys the weird and wonderful but she doesn't feel the need to see orange juice go up Karl Wrenbury's nose. Karl says when he is old enough he will grow a beard and have at least six dogs.

After Karl goes, I am thinking how it would be utterly good if Betty Moody came back.

She would really like Karl Wrenbury, I am sure of it.

Betty and me find completely the same things funny.

If my mother and father were rich and had a butler who could fly a helicopter, then I could buzz over there and collect Betty back from Russia.

Ruby's father, Mr. Redfort, is rich because he is a multimillionaire and Mrs. Redfort is a lady who lunches, which means she doesn't do anything except get her hair washed professionally and have her nails painted in a beauty salon, then she goes to meet her friends for lunch and she says things like, "Darling, how simply divine to see you," and then she comes home and gets changed into an evening gown and goes out for dinner.

And that is simply all she does.

I say, "Mom, how come you don't change into an evening gown for dinner?"

She says, "I do, it's called a bath robe. Now hurry up and get those baked beans down you pronto!"

My life is nothing like Ruby Redfort's.

Chapter 11

On Wednesday, me and Karl are working on our exhibit. It's going to be really good. I'm sure of it.

Toby Hawkling asks Mrs. Wilberton if he can join in with us if he absolutely promises to be strictly properly behaved.

Mrs. Wilberton says, "Not on your nelly, Toby Hawkling." Then she laughs.

I don't like it when Mrs. Wilberton laughs—it gives me the shivers.

Karl is thinking of lots of gadgets and things we can make, and all I have to do is borrow my dad's electrical razor and my mom's powder puffing case, the toaster, and a few other whatnots, and then Karl says he can make them into Ruby Redfort special zappers and walkie-talkies and transmitters and all kinds of other clever things like that.

I don't know how Karl Wrenbury knows all this, because I don't.

He says his dad used to help him before he went off somewhere.

He never came back.

But before that happened, they made lots of useful things together.

Now Karl does them on his own, in the shed.

It's lucky Karl is so clever because Mom is too busy down at the community center to help. She says everyone will have to get their own supper and things because she is still helping Bert find a new place to live.

I know this is important, but so is a cardigan with jam on it needing a wash.

Mom says, "Get Grandad to show you how to use the machine."

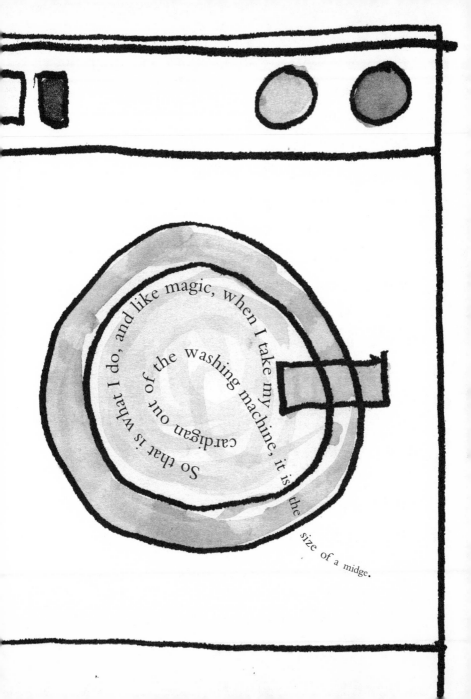

So that is what I do, and like magic, when I take my cardigan out of the washing machine, it is the size of a midge.

Housework isn't really Grandad's strong point—not anymore, not with everything being all technology and everything.

In the old days, laundry meant two hands and a bar of soap and then rubbing.

I have to clean the sink—that is one of my jobs.

Can you imagine Ruby Redfort cleaning a sink?

The answer is NO, because she has Mrs. Digby, who looks after her every need.

Ruby Redfort is too busy solving crimes to clean a sink.

Mom says if I moan about this, she will get me to clean the toilet.

I'm thinking about calling the child protector people.

The difference between my parents and Ruby's parents is Ruby's mother and father give Ruby everything she needs,

which is most things.

And my parents
don't.

Once I have done my cleaning, I go to my room.

I am trying to be alone so I can do some thinking and work out some answers to some big questions.

But the little squirt, Minal, comes barging in and as usual is babbling on about nonsense.

The advantage of being an only child is you could have a room of your own and not be bugged by nincompoops.

Also, I would be more likely to get extra pocket money so I can send off for the new Ruby Redfort underwater lie detector watch, which costs 19.99 dollars!

You can get someone to wear it and it will tell you if they are lying because when they are lying their pulse starts to beat really fast and then the watch beeps!

Betty says it doesn't really work if they have been running because then your pulse always beats really fast.

And then you have to ask yourself, "Have they been running, or are they lying and it might be that they are lying about having been running?"

But how do you know that?

Betty also says it leaks underwater.

Anyway, it's great because it has this picture of Ruby Redfort in the middle, and the actual hands of the watch come out of her nose, and the second hand is a

fly.

The other thing I am wondering about is Betty, and that maybe she is just in Russia on vacation and not kidnapped by aliens, and if she is just on vacation, why didn't she bother to even tell me she was going?

Ruby Redfort was sitting in her special thinking chair on the roof.

Mrs. Digby had made her a super multivitamin drink to help her brain think faster.

While she sipped, she inspected her latest gadget. Control had given it to her when she was summoned to HQ.

The gadget turned out to be rather interesting. It was a tiny backpack that folded out to form a pair of wings just big enough for an eleven-year-old girl. It was a new design, straight from the lab. It meant that if Ruby ever got trapped in a tight spot, high up, say, on top of a building, she could just jump off and glide safely down. Who knew when she might need to do that?

Chapter 12

At school on Thursday, I can't quite believe it, because guess who has appeared out of nowhere? Betty Moody, and she is wearing a hat with earflaps. She says she has been in Russia because her mom, Call-Me-Mol, had a book launching do, and at the absolutely last minute Mol and Cecil thought, What could be better than to take Betty?

Betty said that one hardly ever gets to go to Russia, and that is why, if someone asks you if you want to go, you must say,
utterly
yes.

I can't wait to tell Betty about the book exhibit.

I say, "Guess what our book exhibit is going to be?"

I don't wait for her to guess—I just say, "Ruby Redfort, arch detective!"

Betty says it's a brilliant idea.

And of course, she is right.

Betty says everyone is reading Ruby Redfort in Russia too, and that in Russian she is called something more Russian.

And then Betty says, "You will never believe it but guess who I met in Russia? Patricia F. Maplin Stacey!"

And she's right—I don't believe it.

And then Betty shows me a picture of herself standing next to Patricia F. Maplin Stacey.

Which is proof that it is true.

Patricia F. Maplin Stacey looks nothing like the picture of herself on the back cover. She is much older and she is not wearing a pantsuit.

She is shorter than she is meant to be.

And Betty says, "Yes, that is the strange thing."

Betty says I must come over after school because she has got a present from Russia for me.

I utterly can't wait, but then I remember about how I am supposed to be meeting up with Karl to work on our exhibit.

When I tell Betty, she says, "But why are you paired up with Karl Wrenbury? You are meant to be in a pair with me."

And then I tell her about how it was Mrs. Wilberton and not me who came up with that idea and that I didn't even want to be doing an exhibit with Karl Wrenbury but that it turns out that he is quite good at ideas and that it turns out that he is quite nice and you might not think he would be.

But he is.

Betty says, "But Karl Wrenbury is always being stupid and he will mess everything up."

I say, "But he has come up with some utterly amazing gadgets.

He really has.

And I think you would

really like him.

He is utterly funny

and he can drink orange juice up his nose!"

Betty says,

"Oh well,
if you like Karl Wrenbury so much,
then you can do your stupid Ruby
exhibit with him."

I can't believe what she is saying. Betty
Moody would never call Ruby Redfort stupid.

I say,
"Well, you're the one who
just went off
and didn't even bother to tell me
you were going."

And she says,
"I did too tell you!
I left two messages!
And one message
was from a telephone
in actual Russia!"

And I shout,
"Oh yes?
Well, how come
I didn't get them?"

And she shouts,

"Well, ask your brother Kurt
and your grandad because
I most certainly
did leave messages
and they will tell you
that it's
true.
And I sent you
a postcard from Russia!
And maybe I
shouldn't have
bothered!"

And then Mrs. Wilberton shouts,

"Will you two please pipe down!
We do not tolerate
shouting
at this school."

I want to tell her that she herself is shouting,
but I decide not to.

Betty won't talk to me for all the rest of the day.

We have never had an even slightest argument before.

Except for once when I ate her packed lunch doughnut by accident.

I can't believe it.

It's the most awfullest thing that has ever happened in my whole utter entire life.

I am walking home on my own, filled with gloom.

And I am thinking about the postcard that was—just as I thought—from Betty, and about the message that I found Cement, our dog, eating, which must have been from Betty.

And the message my grandad couldn't remember properly, and that was of course from Betty when she was actually in Russia.

And she is right—

she did try to tell me.

I try to read RUBY REDFORT RULES just to cheer

myself up, but I am feeling almost too full of a gloomy feeling.

"Jeepers, Ruby! What do ya s'pose happened here?"

Ruby Redfort and Clancy Crew were looking at the wreckage that used to be Mr. Crew's study.

His safe had been broken into and all the important top-secret documents it had once contained were gone.

"Looks like you've been burgled," sighed Ruby. "Reckon they found what they were looking for?"

"Never mind what they took. What do you suppose THIS is doing here?"

Clancy Crew was just staring. He didn't know what to think.

He was holding a jacket. It wasn't any old jacket. It was the one that Dirk Draylon always wore in CRAZY COPS.

"Dirk Draylon couldn't have done this, could he, Ruby? I mean, he wouldn't, would he?"

"Nah, I don't think so, Clance. Something's wrong about all this, you know what I mean? I smell a big fat rat. I'll bet you a million milk shakes this is a setup. Someone just wants us to think Dirk Draylon is involved. Oh boy, do I smell a rat."

Chapter 13

On Friday, Mrs. Wilberton has a very livid look on her face and says she has just about had it up to here. She says this time she means business. I am really wondering what she is going on about, and also how she manages to make her eyes go so beady. And I am thinking how she could almost be the evil Count von Viscount in disguise.

They have the same eyebrows, I am sure of it.

I am remembering that bit in RUBY REDFORT SAVES THE DAY, when Ruby is at the ambassador's very important party and there is this old lady there who seems entirely innocent and not remotely dodgy.

And then Ruby Redfort gets one of her suspicions about her and pulls off the lady's face, which is a mask, only to find that it is really Count von Viscount, who is of course livid to be discovered and maybe it is the same with Mrs. Wilberton. Maybe if I—

"Clarice Bean, you seem to be looking very shifty. Perhaps you would like to tell us all what's on your mind?"

Of course I don't think it would be a good idea to tell Mrs. Wilberton that she has the eyebrows of a wicked count.

So I just look sheepish.

Mrs. Wilberton says, "Clarice Bean, I am really not prepared to tell you again, if you cannot be bothered to pay attention to me, then maybe you will pay attention to Mr. Pickering!"

I wait outside Mr. Pickering's office for maybe approximately twenty-three minutes.

I am starting to know how it must feel to be Karl Wrenbury.

I am just staring at a poster that says

DANGERS IN THE HOME

and then has a picture of a lady standing on a rickety stool, changing a light bulb, while she is being distracted by a small baby, who is playing with a pair of scissors.

Karl Wrenbury must have looked at this poster a lot.

Finally, Mrs. Marse says, "Mr. Pickering is occupied with important business. He will not have time to tell you off."

So I go back to my classroom.

What Mrs. Wilberton is up in arms about is that, "Someone, and I've got a pretty good idea who you are, has stolen the book exhibit winners' cup."

Karl Wrenbury is instantly sent home!

Mrs. Wilberton says it must be him because, quite frankly, it always is.

Also he was seen loitering around the trophy shelf where the cup is always kept.

And now it is missing and you don't have to be a genius to work out what happened.

Mrs. Wilberton says Karl will not be allowed to take part in the competition because he has reached a level of naughtiness that will not be tolerated.

I am utterly beside myself because now I might be disqualified from the competition.

And I have lost two exhibit partners in a row. And if I am not careful, I will end up being in a pair with Toby Hawkling.

Chapter 14

I have an utterly dreary and miserablish Weekend because my best friend, Betty Moody, is not being best friends with me anymore.

And when I go over to Karl Wrenbury's house, he says he can't be bothered to finish the Ruby model since he is disqualified.

Karl Wrenbury says, "It's not fair because I didn't even do it."

I say, "Oh really?"

He says, "Why would I steal the cup when I thought we were going to win it?"

Quite a good point actually.

The other thing is, Karl Wrenbury never says he hasn't done something bad because he is utterly proud of his wicked ways.

So he is obviously not the culprit.

All I know is, now I am definitely not going to win. I have no Ruby gadgets, only half of a not-finished model and, for a start, I can't think of a learning thing to do with our exhibit. I haven't even made my Ruby badges, and they were going to be utterly popular. I am thinking about giving up.

When I get back home, I telephone my granny. I tell her all about the missing cup and how Karl most likely didn't do it and is in deep troubling water for a crime he didn't commit, and that everything is

dreadfully suspicious and

utterly wrong.

I say, "It just doesn't add up, Granny."

Which is exactly what Ruby Redfort would say if she had to solve this crime.

And Granny says, "If Karl didn't do it, then somebody else must have, and the big question is who?"

I say, "Yes, who?"

And Granny says, "Mrs. Pinkerton!"

I say, "Who's Mrs. Pinkerton? I don't think there's anyone called Mrs. Pinkerton at my school."

And Granny says, "No, no. I am meant to be over, playing cards, at Mrs. Pinkerton's—I'm late!"

She says, "I will have to go, but Clarice, maybe you could solve the mystery."

I say,

"But how can I?

I'm not a

mystery solver."

Granny says, "You must have learned something about solving a mystery after reading all those Ruby Redfort detective books.

"Let me know how you get on."

I sit for ages thinking about what Granny has just said, and the more I think about it, the more I think she is right.

I must have learned lots about being a mystery solver from Ruby Redfort, and if I can solve this mystery, then I can prove Karl Wrenbury is not the cup stealer.

And if I can prove he is not the cup stealer, then I can prove that I have learned something from reading the Ruby Redfort books, which Mrs. Wilberton likes to call drivel, when in fact they are packed with good advice and clever useful information.

I nip straight upstairs.

The first thing is, you have to make a list. That's what Ruby always does.

She has a special tiny computer to write on. But it is not utterly necessary to have one, which I don't.

Also, you do not need a magnifying glass, because that is old-fashioned.

Just your wits and a pen and a smallish piece of paper.

Then you write down all the clues.

The most important clues are the people you are suspicious about.

They are called the suspects.

My mainly suspects would be Mrs. Wilberton and Grace Grapello.

Mrs. Wilberton probably didn't do it, even though I would like it to be her. All evidence points to it being Grace Grapello because she is probably highly jealous of our idea and desperate to have a good one of her own, but can't. Toby Hawkling is my thirdish suspect, because it's always good to have three people on your list.

Three is normal for suspects.

Robert Granger isn't a suspect because he would never have thought of it.

He never thinks of anything on his own without copying someone else and also he is a goody-goody.

The other thing I have to write down is just when did they find the cup was missing????

No one has seen it on the trophy shelf since Mr. Skippard did his spring clean-up. So for all anybody knows, it could have been stolen before, when the boys' toilets got flooded, over nearly two weeks ago.

This starts me thinking, and then I get stuck, so I do a bit more reading.

Ruby Redfort was thinking hard.

What did it all mean? She felt this might be a good time to talk things over with her good friend, Clancy Crew. Clancy had a way of figuring things out.

He was very bright.

She dialed the number.

"Hi, Clance, how you doing?"

"Is that you, Ruby? I was hoping you would call. I am stuck here at this boring dinner. My dad is entertaining all these celebrities and government people and boy, is it a yawn."

Clancy Crew's father was ambassador and was always inviting very important, top-notch guests for dinner. He liked to come across as a family man and insisted that all five of his children always attend these social functions.

"Do you think you might be able to slip away?" asked Ruby.

"Not a chance. Could you maybe make it over here?"

It was Hitch's night off, and there was no one to drive her over to Clancy's house, but that was OK — she could ride her bike.

Of course, Ruby Redfort's bike was no ordinary bike and was fitted with a phone, a rocket booster, and an anti-attack repeller.

"I'll be there in five," said Ruby, and climbed out of her bedroom window.

The person I really want to talk to is Betty
Moody, but she isn't talking to me.

I tell Mom how
  everything is ruined,
and that Betty and me are
      not utterly best friends
anymore.
And how it will never be the same again.
              Never not ever.

Mom says, "I think you are being a little
bit dramatic. If Betty isn't talking to you, then
maybe you should go and talk to her. Real friends
don't let some tiny little argument get in the way.
If they did, then no one would be talking
to anybody."

She says, "Why don't you see if Betty would
like to come over for supper? We might have
hot dogs."

I walk very slowly because I feel a bit sick—
I am anxiously worrying that Betty Moody

will shut the front door in my face.

I ring the doorbell. It's not a normal doorbell, of course.

The Moodys brought it back from the Far East. It is made of wood tubes and makes a woody sound.

Our doorbell only works from time to time— you never know when.

Betty Moody herself actually answers the door. She is wearing furry slipper boots. I expect they are Russian.

She says, "Hello, Clarice Bean," as if nothing is wrong, although she is fidgeting quite a bit.

I say, "Hello, Betty, would you like to come over for supper? We will be probably having hot dogs."

Betty says, "Will Karl Wrenbury be there?"

I say, "Utterly no."

Betty says, "All right, I'll come over at six."

Then I go home feeling slightly a bit better.

Although I notice she doesn't give me my present from Russia.

When I get home, I almost get knocked over in my own hallway by the several dogs we now have.

They are barking like mad, and Mom says she is at her wits' end.

Dad says he has never been so eager to go back to work in his life.

Mom says Grandad had better find somewhere
to put them all, i.e., not in this house.

I go into the kitchen, and there is Chloë
Brownling.

She is one of Marcie's friends, which is odd
because Marcie is out and not here and it is
just Kurt and Chloë on their own,
with each other
    alone.
      Sitting awfully closely.
             And Kurt
               is making her
                 a cup of
                   herbally tea,

and he is talking and saying things like
"Would you like a toasted muffin?" and
"I like your hair that way—it really suits you."

Of course, I am astonished.

When I tell Mom about it she says, "Yes, Chloë
is Kurt's new girlfriend. I think he really likes
her."

She says, "Kurt is a lot better now he has
a reason to wash, but Marcie is worse than ever."

Mom says, "Marcie isn't talking to Kurt because
she feels Kurt has stolen her friend. And Kurt isn't
talking to Marcie because Marcie told Chloë that
Kurt's room smells of cheese." Which is true.

Mom says, "For goodness sake! Why can't
people just get along?"

When Chloë sees Flossie, who is of course the
German shepherd, she screams like a maniac,
which just makes things utterly worse.

All the dogs start loudly barking.

And Chloë says she can't come over anymore

because she is utterly terrified of German shepherds. And isn't really a dog person, full stop.

Kurt goes into a decline. He says, "I hate living here sometimes."

Dad says, "I know how you feel—this house is going to the dogs."

Mom gives him a look.

Then Mrs. Stampney comes over. She is in curlers and fed up to the back teeth. She says she is trying to have a relaxing bath but it is hard to relax when there are three howling dogs on the other side of the wall. She says this is a disturbance to the peace and her nerves are literally frayed.

She says she is making a complaint to the police station about us.

Mom says she would be quite happy to drive her over there.

Then the doorbell rings and it is Karl Wrenbury. He says, "Sit!" and all the dogs sit, and he says, "Quiet!" and all the dogs are quiet.

He says he has dogs at home, and he spends
most of his time training them.

His mom is a dog walker, and he has learned
quite a bit about dog obedience. Mom says she is
very grateful and would he like to stay for
hot dogs?

And Karl says, "Yes,
please." But of course, it is
an utter disaster when I
remember that Betty Moody
is coming over. What will
she say when she sees
Karl Wrenbury? She
might never forgive
me.

At that moment, the
doorbell rings again.

It only goes slightly
PING because it has
lost the PONG bit,
which is a pity.

Ruby Redfort has a doorbell that plays a tune.

When I open the door, it's Betty Moody.

She sees the dogs and she goes utterly over the

moon.

Betty Moody loves dogs but the Moodys can

never ever have one because they are always

leaving the country at the drop of a hat.

And you
can't just take
a dog with
you whenever
you feel like it.
Which I suppose
is why we never go
anywhere.
Karl shows Betty how
to make
them sit
and beg.

He says, if she wants, she can come over and walk his dogs sometimes after school.

Mom says, "You are welcome to borrow these two if you want to see what it's like to own some." She is joking but Betty phones Mol and Cecil anyway and asks them if she can look after Flossie and Ralph, just for one, maybe two weeks until Bert can find a new old folks' home that's equipped for taking pets.

And Mol says it might be very good for Betty to experience the responsibility of looking after an animal.

And so the answer is maybe yes. Mom says, "Thank goodness for that."

Kurt goes to call Chloë, and Betty decides Karl isn't so bad after all.

Chapter 15

On Monday, back at school, Karl and Betty are chattering nonstop about dogs.

Betty seems to have forgotten all about not

liking Karl Wrenbury and calling him a super limpet.

When I ask her, she says she never didn't like him—she just didn't want him messing everything up for us and our exhibit.

She says, "If he is going to be a helpful influence, then he can certainly be in our pair."

The only problem is Karl is not allowed to do the exhibit because he is still

in trouble

for stealing the little cup.

And although I have been working on a gadget thingy of my own, Karl was doing the best bit of the exhibit, and I am worried it is going to be a disaster without him.

Betty says, "In any case, we can't win the competition if we can't think of anything that we have learned from Ruby Redfort. And that's the problem—we can't."

I say, "But that is what I have been meaning to tell you.

"I think we can solve the crime and win the cup because it turns out that we have learned quite a lot from Ruby Redfort."

I tell Betty Moody what my plan is and she says she "will definitely help." And "wow, how exciting."

We are interviewing everyone about what they know, and what they don't know, and what they don't know they know.

That's something that Clancy Crew always says. He says, "Sometimes people don't even know what they know because they haven't really thought about it. But if they did, they would realize they knew more than they thought they knew."

I think I know what he means.

We ask Alexandra Holker.

I say we are investigating the missing cup . . . and when exactly it went missing, i.e., maybe it was stolen just after the boys' toilets got flooded.

And Alexandra says, "You know what, Clarice

Bean? I think you might be on to something."
Which is weird because that's just what Clancy
Crew would say.

I ask her what she thinks about the culprit
perhaps being Grace Grapello. And she says,
"Well, the thing is, Grace Grapello was away with
a germy flu bug and so was not there when we
think the actual little cup went missing."

Of course she is right.

I say, "What about Toby Hawkling? Do you
think he did it?"

And Alexandra says, "No, not really, because
Toby Hawkling never does anything without Karl
Wrenbury telling him to."

And of course, she is right.

I say, "What about Mrs. Wilberton? Do you
think she stole the cup?"

And she says, "No."

I say, "What makes you think that?"

And she says, "Because she is the teacher."

Alexandra Holker would be a really good

detective because she has a really good memory for details and that is a must if you are going to be a detective.

So if it's not Mrs. Wilberton, and not Grace Grapello, and not Toby Hawkling, just who is it? We can't think of anyone, and all our clues are adding up to make one big zero, which is what Ruby says sometimes to her butler, Hitch.

And what Hitch often says is, "Sometimes you just have to look at things

sideways

and then

you get

a clearer picture."

I'm not sure what that means, but when we get back to the Moodys' house, we ask Mol and she says, "I think what Hitch means is, if you think about something in a different way, then sometimes it's easier to find the answer."

She says, "What you have to think about is why would anyone steal the cup in the first place? There's no point having the winners' cup if it doesn't have your name written on it

saying

Winner

and there's no point having it at all if you can't show it to everybody on parents' night."

She says, "Maybe if you think about the cup as being lost rather than stolen, then perhaps you just might find it."

Mol is really clever at these things because she is a crime writer.

Her whole life is about puzzling things out.

Chapter 16

On Tuesday, Betty Moody
and I are busy searching for
the cup.

We look everywhere, even outside
in the giant bins with wheels. We
give up after Betty nearly falls in.
We have to get Mr. Skippard to
rescue Betty's glasses, which have
unfortunately slipped off her nose,
into the trash.

Mr. Skippard is quite annoyed and
says he has better things to do than
climb in and out of Dumpsters. He says
if it happens again, he will have a good
mind to confiscate Betty Moody's glasses
and keep them in his closet.

Mr. Skippard wouldn't really do that
because he is not as mean as he wants
you to think he is.

But it gives me a good idea.

155

You see, one of the places we haven't looked is in Mr. Skippard's actual closet of cleaning equipment, and the cup could maybe perhaps have gotten in there by accident when Mr. Skippard was doing his spring clean-up.

Betty says, "It's a long shot, but it's worth a try."

Which is what Clancy Crew says in every single story.

Very unfortunately indeed, Betty Moody and me get caught red-handed, clattering about in Mr. Skippard's closet.

Mr. Skippard is definitely extremely upset. He says, "The janitor's closet is absolutely off limits and totally out of bounds for all pupils. And that is final."

Even more utterly unfortunately, Mrs. Wilberton is passing by when Mr. Skippard is telling us off and then we are in big trouble.

Mrs. Wilberton says, "Well, Clarice Bean, I am not so surprised by this wilfully disgraceful lack of good conduct." Whatever that means. "But as for you, Betty Moody, I am sorry but I really thought you had more sense."

She says, "Well, since the two of you like closets so much, you can both stay in during recess and stack all the books on MY closet shelves."

Of course, this is a nuisance because we are trying to solve a mystery.

And we have got more important things to do than sort things out for someone beginning with W who is too lazy to clear up her own closet. It takes us ages to do it because we are taking turns to read RUBY REDFORT RULES out loud to each other.

After negotiating her way through countless winding corridors and climbing endless flights of stone stairs, Ruby Redfort arrived at a steel door. She felt certain that this must be the door behind which the unfortunate celebrity was being held.

Ruby picked the lock without much difficulty, and there, looking just a little bemused, was Dirk Draylon.

"Boy, am I glad to see you," sighed Dirk. "I didn't think I was ever gonna get outta here."

"Don't worry, Dirk. I'll get you out," whispered Ruby as she untied the weary TV star.

"You take my glider wings. They are designed only to take the weight of an eleven-year-old girl, but you look like you've lost a lot of pounds, Dirk, and hey, we don't have much choice."

"But what about you?"

"Don't worry about me, Dirk. I'll be just fine."

"I owe you big time, kid," he said, before jumping from the tiny window and floating the 600-and-something feet to the ground below.

It was at that moment Ruby heard a chilling voice behind her.

"So we meet again, Ruby Redfort—arch interferer and tiresome schoolgirl. You really think you can outwit the evil genius Count von Viscount, do you?"

"Well, I thought I would give it a go," joked Ruby, trying to sound relaxed although her heart was beating so fast she could barely breathe.

"Well, since you are here, I might as well tell you my little idea. It's incredibly clever."

Betty is reading away when I accidentally knock something off the shelf I am tidying, and it hits her on the head.

You'll
utterly never believe it,
but it's the tiny cup.

What is it doing in Mrs. Wilberton's closet is what I want to know.

Just then, Mrs. Wilberton calls out, "Clarice Bean, Betty, will you please come out of that closet and sit down."

And I say, "Mrs. Wilberton, I didn't know that there were two cups for the book exhibit winners."

And she says, "Well, that is because there aren't."

I say, "But Mrs. Wilberton, there's a little cup in your closet and it looks just exactly like the little cup for the winner of the exhibit. You know, like the little cup that Karl Wrenbury has stolen."

And when Mrs. Wilberton sees the cup, she goes as red as an actual beetroot, and then she beetles off to see Mr. Pickering.

She doesn't come back for ages.

It turns out that Mrs. Wilberton asked Mr. Skippard to give the cup a bit of a polish to get it ready for parents' night. She said to put it away safely on the trophy shelf, but there was a mix-up because Mr. Skippard thought Mrs. Wilberton meant safely on her closet shelf since she would be needing it on this actual Wednesday, but Mrs. Wilberton meant safely on the glass trophy shelf.

On my way out of school, I hear Mrs. Marse say, "Mr. Pickering was absolutely livid and said to Mrs. Wilberton that she cannot go around blaming people willy-nilly for things they didn't do."

And then Mr. Skippard says, "I couldn't agree more."

Betty comes over to my house after school. When we get in, Mom is in quite a good mood because she has found an old persons' home that will take a larger pet than merely a bird or a fish.

But you may only have just the one dog, i.e., Flossie or Ralph.

That is the catch.

Bert says he couldn't do without Flossie because they have been each other's companion for nearly over eleven years, which, if you are a dog, is seventy-seven years.

And that is the same age as Bert himself. He says, "We are both senior citizens." Ralph is much younger, and in dog years, is more the same age as my dad.

If Ralph was a human being, then he would probably have been in the same class as my dad and I expect they could have been friends.

Before supper, me, Betty Moody, Mom, Grandad, and Bert go to look around the new old folks' home.

We all have to squish in the car.

It is called Sunset Homes, which Betty and me think sounds utterly romantic.

It is all painted the most extremely bright colors and there's a poster in the entrance hall that says,

YOU DON'T HAVE TO BE NUTS TO WORK HERE, BUT IT HELPS!

Mom says why Sunset Homes is so nice is because they have such a good sense of humor. It's family run, which means all the people who work there are from the same entire family. They all wear glasses.

Can you imagine my family running an old folks' home together?

Because I can't.

The lady in charge, called Pam, says the thing is, Sunset Homes understands how important it is for people to have their personal pets with them. She says she only wishes Sunset Homes could take more animals, but if they took every single person's pet, it would end up more like a farm than a residence for the elderly.

Bert is quite taken with it, especially when he sees apple brown Betty on the menu. Which, for me, is my worst utter dessert. You could probably only get me to eat it if you gave me approximately twenty-seven dollars.

Bert says the only thing he is anxious about is what will happen to Ralph, the Pekingese? He couldn't bear for him to be unhappy.

Betty says, "I'll look after him! We really love Ralph, and we would really love him to be living with us on a full-time basis in our house, and I think Ralph really does like us.

"I have seen him smiling, which is hard to see on a dog, but I have.

"And he is always following my dad around and sometimes he just stares at him and listens to him playing the piano.

"I think he is musical, and he has probably never had a piano before, and we do, and he can listen to it whenever he likes. He really can.

"And we will bring him to visit you

whenever you like, Bert, we really will."

Bert is really pleased with this idea but Mom says we must ask Cecil and Mol first.

And what will happen to Ralph when the Moodys go away?

And Betty says Karl Wrenbury will look after him because his mother is a professional dog looker-afterer.

We phone Mol and Cecil utterly right away at once.

And they say, "Yes!"

It's been such an exciting day. Almost like the kind of days Ruby Redfort has. And now I can't wait to read about how Ruby will escape from the evil genius Count von Viscount. Because you can bet she will.

"Well, it looks like the end of the road for you, Ruby Redfort, child DEFECTIVE.

"Within twenty minutes, this whole room will be flooded in water. Let's see you get out of that one! I don't THINK so! Ah ha ha ha!" With that, the wicked Count turned and sealed the door shut.

It was then that Ruby remembered her little laser disguised as a decorative piece of jewelry. Ruby got to work. Within seconds she had cut through the steel handcuffs and was trying to unlock the metal door, but it just wouldn't budge. Even the tiny window was securely blocked and impossible to open. The room was fast filling with water. There seemed to be no escape . . . until, in desperation, she looked up, and there, quite unexpectedly, she saw a tiny trapdoor—just big enough for an eleven-year-old girl to squeeze through.

There was just the small problem of oxygen and breathing underwater. She did have her miniature diving apparatus, but would it give her enough time?

Chapter 17

Finally, it is Wednesday,
the big day of parents' night,
and it is all extremely
exciting and everything.
Everybody has set up their tables.

Ours is looking marvelous
because we have the best exhibit.
It is a smoking volcano that actually
smokes. We aren't going to turn it on
until the last minute so it is more of a surprise.

Also, we don't want it to run out
of smoke before the judges get to see it.

Karl has made a little helicopter
and Betty and me have made little models
of Clancy Crew and Ruby Redfort. Count
von Viscount has got them dangling over
the volcano. I made Count von Viscount. He is
papier-mâché, which is just soggy newspaper
with paste. It takes quite a lot of work to do.

The hard part is waiting for it
to dry. But it is worth it.
Karl has made a tape of the chilling
laugh—which is really in actual fact
Mrs. Wilberton's but she doesn't know it.

Noah and Suzie Woo have got an actual wok in their exhibit, which is a bit like a frying pan, but not.

It's just for show—they are not actually allowed to do any cooking in it in case it is a fire hazard. But they have made sushi, which is fish not cooked, wrapped around a blob of rice.

And they have a display of bananas, which are not bananas but called plantains and are more like a potato pretending to be a banana.

After a little bit of looking around, everybody does their speech.

I do my speech in the style of Ruby Redfort. Which is utterly clever.

So it sounds really good.

I say, "What I have learned from the Ruby Redfort books is a lot."

Then I describe how we put all the clues together and one and one made two, and they all added up to mean the cup was not stolen, but just someone had been utterly forgetful, naming no names, and then blamed the wrong person. Which sometimes happens if you jump to conclusions.

And then I say, "And it is amazing what you can learn from any books you enjoy, and you don't necessarily realize you are learning something because you are so busy enjoying it."

Of course, everyone claps.

Mrs. Wilberton is smiling and staring and clapping a bit too much.

And Mr. Pickering says, "Nice work, girls!" Which is a bit like at the end of the Ruby Redfort books, when Hitch always says, "Nice work, kid."

Mr. Pickering says, "It's thanks to you two that we have got the cup in time for this evening. I really am very impressed with your detective work.

"You could have that Ruby Redfort out of a job if she's not careful!"

Which is nice of him to say, but not true because Ruby Redfort is not an actual real-life person.

But I wish she was.

I give him one of our Ruby badges, which are homemade.

And he wears it.

It says, OH BOY, WHAT A YAWN!

Anyway, everyone thinks our speech is dreadfully entertaining and Call-Me-Mol says, "Brilliant, girls!"

Karl's mother says she is so relieved she won't have to discuss Karl's bad behavior tonight.

And Mr. Pickering says so is he.

And Mrs. Wilberton has to say she is awfully apologetic for the mishap.

She gives Karl a box of jelly beans as a "sorry."

After everyone has done their speech about the learning part of their exhibit, the parents go around looking at all the models and things.

I hear Mrs. Wilberton say to Robert Granger and Arnie Singh, "It's a very nicely made exhibit, Robert and Arnie, but perhaps you should stick a little more closely to the facts." She says, "There were no chicken dinosaurs."

That is a fact.

"These bones are not sixty-five million years old."

That is also a fact.

I notice that Robert and Arnie do not take any notice of Mrs. Wilberton, and as soon as the parents come around, they tell them all the whole nonsense of how they found the dinosaur chicken bones in Robert's backyard.

Grace Grapello throws up because she eats most of Alexandra Holker's Victorian fudges without asking.

They are meant to be for the visitors.

She is too ill to do her exhibit of ballet with Cindy Fisher.

Toby Hawkling was meant to be doing the ballet too, but he got an unfortunate tummy bug in the morning and says he is not allowed to do anything that involves twirling or he might faint.

It doesn't stop him from eating eight egg sandwiches, though.

Cindy has to do the performance on her own. It's not very good because Cindy Fisher has only been going to ballet for maybe two weeks and she doesn't even know the moves.

She makes most of it up.

Grace Grapello has to go home early.

Mrs. Wilberton says, "It seems to me, Grace Grapello, that you got your just desserts."

Lots of people I know are at parents' night, even Bert, Flossie, and Ralph, and also my dad.

Normally Dad is too busy at the office and can't get away because Mr. Thorncliff is always breathing down his neck.

Mr. Thorncliff is a very strict boss and he does not like people having time off to enjoy themselves.

Dad told Miss Egglington, his secretary, who you must not call a secretary but instead a personal assistant, to tell Mr. Thorncliff that he had

gone home early with a case of the food poisoning.

Which is funny because after some of Noah and Suzie Woo's sushi, he actually really does feel a bit iffy.

I show Dad our exhibit and Karl lights the smoking volcano and nothing at all happens for almost nearly one minute.

It is very thrilling.

We are on tiptoes waiting.

And then gradually there is a puff of smoke. It looks utterly realistically like an actual volcano. It smells a bit funny, but volcanoes do, I should think.

We will probably almost definitely win.

Then Mr. Pickering comes on the loudspeaker. He says, "Please join me in the assembly hall, where I will be announcing the winner of this year's book competition."

He does a little talk.

Which I forget to concentrate on halfway through because I am watching a spider dangling down, almost just about to land on Mr. Pickering's head.

Luckily, I come back into concentration just in time to hear him say, "Without further ado, the winner is . . ."

I close my eyes and wait to hear my name but when I open them again the little cup is being awarded to Alexandra Holker because, Mr. Pickering says, "She came up with a very informative exhibit, and to act out so much of the Victorian age in just a few minutes was very ambitious."

And that, "Not everyone would be able to be Queen Victoria one minute and Charles Dickens the next."

And also, "What was left of the Victorian fudge was very good indeed."

We are utterly **disappointed** not to be the winners and not to be awarded the tiny cup, and also not the mystery prize either.

At least it was Alexandra who won it, who I like, and not Grace Grapello, who I don't.

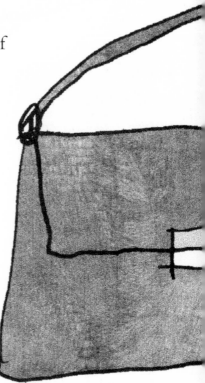

The mystery prize turns out to be not so mysterious after all and is typical of what Mrs. Wilberton would choose.

It is called The Encyclopaedia of Ballet,

which is only a good prize if
you are fascinated by
ballet, which
I
am
not.
While
everybody
is busy watching
Alexandra winning,
Karl Wrenbury's
smoking volcano gets
caught on fire and sets the
sprinklers off.
Mrs. Wilberton goes
stark staring mad.
She says her suede-look
handbag
is
ruined.

I must say, the egg sandwiches for all the guests are not eatable.

Luckily, the tiny sausages on sticks are fine.

When my uncle Ted, who is a firefighter, turns up, he says, "It's not really wise to have anything smoking in a classroom. Not without the correct level of supervision."

Mrs. Wilberton is called into Mr. Pickering's office. I think she gets a telling-off. I hope so.

Karl Wrenbury is sent home. And so is everybody else.

Chapter 18

On Thursday I wake up really early, even though school has been cancelled due to water in the classroom causing a day off, and Mr. Skippard having to mop it all up.

He will have to wear rain boots.

I heard Mr. Skippard say to Mrs. Marse, "Mrs. Wilberton can wave bye-bye to those carpet tiles in her reading corner."

Because of course they are utterly soaking wet. And I heard Mrs. Marse say, "Quite honestly, that's the least of her problems."

I am going to call Granny and tell her about all the goings-on just as soon as I have read the last ever page in my book, RUBY REDFORT RULES. I almost don't want to finish it, but I utterly want to know how it turns out.

That's the thing that sometimes happens when you read a really good book—

you just

want to

read

it

all

over

a

g

a i n.

Ruby Redfort walked out of HQ and climbed into the waiting limousine.

What a day it had been—first rescuing her hero, Dirk Draylon, then escaping from the evil genius Count von Viscount, foiling his dastardly plan to take over the world, as usual.

HQ was pleased with Ruby's work and told her to take the rest of the day off.

It was a shame she couldn't make it back to school in time to win the class election but hey, she had been a little tied up. Even Ruby Redfort couldn't win 'em all.

At least Vapona Begwell wouldn't be elected president. Mrs. Drisco had seen to that when she caught Vapona voting for herself more than once.

Using her big toe, Ruby flicked on the super-deluxe wrap-around sound TV.

The show was CRAZY COPS, starring her new friend, Dirk Draylon.

It was quite something to have rescued

everybody's favorite TV celebrity from certain death, and it was only a pity Ruby had forgotten to ask Dirk for an autograph.

Just then, a voice came on the car intercom; it was Hitch.

All he said was,

"Nice work, kid!"

The End

I have **utterly** just finished
the last ever sentence
when our doorbell rings.

It does a strange buzz because the battery needs
to be changed.

I am really hoping it is not Mrs. Stampney or
Robert Granger.

I peek
through
the
mail slot,
just in case.
I can
just
see
Ralph
the Pekingese,

so I open the door.

Luckily he is with Betty Moody.

He looks really happy.

Betty has got him a new collar.

Also, she has got my present that is from Russia.

She can't wait for me to open it.

She is hopping and so is Ralph.

You will never guess what, but it is the utterly newest Ruby Redfort edition.

Betty says it is

"hot off the press,"

which

means

utterly

just

printed

probably

last

week.

It's called RUSH TO RUSSIA, RUBY!
It has a white cover and Ruby Redfort is wearing a furry hat with earflaps, and it's not even in stores yet, and Betty got it from Patricia F. Maplin Stacey herself in person, and Patricia F. Maplin Stacey even wrote in it in felt-tip.

It says:

To Clarice Bean
Keep on reading, Kid!
Love from
Patricia F. Maplin Stacy

Which is exactly the kind of thing Hitch would say.

Turn the page for a sneak peek at
Clarice Bean's next adventure —
Clarice Bean Spells Trouble!

Available August 2005!

Things
you can't Explain—like
why isn't YOU
spelled U?

You might want to know why I did what I did.
But if you were me, you would understand that
sometimes I just don't know why I do things.

So it's hard to explain.

I just get this urge to do something and I do it.

And before I know it, I am in very big trouble.

My mom is always telling me I must think before I
open my mouth and then perhaps life would be a lot
easier.

She is probably right.

But try telling my brain that;
*   it doesn't think as fast as me.*

Another thing that is difficult to explain is
   why YOU isn't spelled U
      and why WHY isn't spelled Y.
Spelling. Who knows where it all came from and why it has to be so difficult. Whoever thought it up must be a very strange person.

You see, it all started with this spelling bee that my teacher, Mrs. Wilberton, organized. It's to see who is the best out of all the spellers.

I am not a good speller; my mind just doesn't have the room in it to remember spellings.

It isn't my fault; it really isn't.

Think of all the other things in your whole life that you want to remember. Like that joke my brother Kurt told me once about the cow on the telephone.

And one time when we went on vacation and it rained like mad and we all got soaked through to our underwear, including everyone.

So spellings are not that important to me.

Compared to these other things, which are.

Anyway, what I am telling you is: spelling causes trouble.

For example, the thing that everyone said I did, the thing that got me into some very big trouble, mainly happened because of spelling.

Someone who is a good speller but is in nonstop trouble is Karl Wrenbury.

Karl Wrenbury is this boy in my class.

You have probably heard of him—most people have. He gets up to no good, but I don't think it's his fault really.

He has just got this zingy thing in him.

He can't control it.

And sometimes he lets the guinea pigs out on purpose.

I like Karl Wrenbury.

At first I didn't and then I got to know him, and then I did.

But he is the naughtiest person in the school, and the problem with knowing the naughtiest person is that then people think you are just as bad.

Why even try to be good?

This is something I have been finding out for myself at home.

My younger brother, Minal, has the knack of learning from my mistakes and avoiding trouble.

This mainly works by getting me into trouble.

I feel like I am turning into Karl Wrenbury.

I am in nonstop trouble these days, which isn't fair, of course.

What happens is, Minal always goes something like, "Mo-o-om, Clarice just really pinched me on the elbow!"

And of course this is utterly not true—and if it is, it was for a very good reason.

And Mom says, "I am too busy and I have too big a headache to be dealing with two unpleasant children. Either continue this argument on another planet or keep out of each other's way."

She isn't always like this—just when she has "had it up to here!"

Which lately she has.

My dad is different. He likes to sort things out. He

is good at that. It's part of his job and he has to do it every day at work.

Dad will not have squabbling.

Absolutely not.

He says, "You can agree to disagree by all means, you can discuss it, or you can change the subject."

But what my dad says you may not do is have two squealy voices driving him utterly around the bend.

Someone who is easily driven around the bend is my older sister, Marcie—she spends most of her time being crabby, and when she isn't being crabby, she is in the bathroom talking on the phone.

My brother Kurt is the oldest out of all of us, and he is mainly in his room not talking to anybody.

❋ ❋ ❋

So now if you still don't understand why it's hard for someone like me to avoid trouble, you should try having Mrs. Wilberton as your teacher. Because if you are in Mrs. Wilberton's class and you are named

Clarice Bean, you might as well face it: trouble is your middle name.

It's just how the cookie gets crumbled.

And I tell you, no one has ever gotten in more trouble in Mrs. Wilberton's class than I did last summer.

Who Decides
What's Important
and What Isn't

Tuesday is not my favorite day because there is
testing to see how smart everyone is and how can
you see that in a test?

That's the thing about school: they might only
test you for one thing, i.e.,

math

or spellingy type things

or punctuationy thingummybobs,

and they will not see that maybe you will know
absolutely every episode of the Ruby Redfort
series by heart. And that you can tell them how
Ruby managed to jump out of a moving
helicopter without twisting an ankle.

Which is a hard thing to do.

And maybe you will know how to cleverly mend your hem with a stapler

or stand on your actual head—

or stand on your actual head while drawing a dog in ballpoint pen—

or teach your *dog* how to draw with a ballpoint pen while *he* stands on *your* head.

But they do not test you for these things because the people who come up with the testing do not think it is important.

But would you rather know someone who knows how to jump out of a moving helicopter without getting a twisted ankle or someone who can spell *grapefruit*?

I would like to know someone who knows how to get green marker out of a white carpet.

Until I do, Betty says put a chair over it.

I just hope my mom doesn't move the chairs before I discover the answer.

Anyway, testing is my worst, whereas someone like Grace Grapello, for an actual example, is good in a test situation because ask her what 3.3 divided by 2.4 is [*] and she will get a big check mark and I will get a headache.

Anyway, there we are doing this testing thing and the room is all quiet and I can just hear the clock ticking really slowly—but strangely, every minute I look up, it is ten minutes later and time is running out.

And I can hear Robert Granger breathing. That's what he does. He sits behind me and breathes.

It drives me utterly crazy.

And I turn around and go, "Stop breathing, will you!"

And he says, "Clarice Bean, of course I cannot stop breathing, because then I would be dead, and how would you like that?"

I decide not to answer his question because

[*] $3.3 \div 2.4 = 1.375$

Mom has taught me if you can't think of anything nice to say, then sometimes it is better to say nothing at all. You see, I am trying really hard to keep it zipped in class, and I don't even utter a single word when I hear Grace Grapello telling Cindy Fisher that I am a duh-brain because I spelled *photo* with an *f*.

Mrs. Wilberton didn't tell her *off* even; she just said, "Clarice Bean, your spelling leaves a lot to be desired."

Anyway, at the end, when time is up, I hand in my test and Mrs. Wilberton says,

"Oh deary dear,

it looks as if a spider has been dipped in ink and struggled across the page!"

I wish someone would dip *her* in ink.

Then she says, "I have some exciting news. I have arranged for the whole school to take part in a spelling bee."

 *Spelling bee* ※ is just a fancy way of saying *test,* but you have to stand there in front of the whole school and spell words out loud on the spot without writing them down. It is interesting that for Mrs. Wilberton giving a spelling test is the most fun she can ever have and for me it is a very good reason to tell Mrs. Marse, the school secretary, that I have a terrible case of a tummy upset and I need to go home as soon as possible, on the double, don't even bother to call my mom.

Anyway, I have been wondering, who is the person who gets to decide what is important?

Because I wish it was me.

※ ※ ※

In the playground, Karl Wrenbury is throwing water balloons at Toby Hawkling. He gets Grace Grapello by accident and she goes off to tell. She is mad because he has gotten her rain

---

※ *Bee,* as in *spelling bee,* means lots of people all working on the same thing at once, like bees all making honey together.

jacket all wet, even though this is what rain jackets are for.

But that's Grace Grapello for you.

She is someone who I don't get along with because she is a know-it-all and a meany and her favorite thing is to tell on people.

I am trying really hard not to get in her way because I don't want to get in a tussle with Mrs. Wilberton and the thing is, Mrs. Wilberton always believes Grace and not me.

But after school I am collecting my coat from my peg and so is Karl and he is telling me a joke about a pig who crosses the road and before he can tell the last bit of it, the actual funny bit, Mrs. Wilberton walks by and says, "Now, move along, you two, before you get into mischief."

You see, Karl gets in trouble even when he is being well behaved.

This is one of the side effects of bad behavior.

And I say, "We were just getting our coats on, Mrs. Wilberton."

And she says, "No answering back, thank you very much."

I say, "Excuse me for breathing," but I say it really really quietly.

✳ ✳ ✳

I go home in a very downcast-ish mood, and even my older brother, Kurt, says, "What's the matter with you?" which is unusual, because usually he doesn't notice other people's gloom—he is too busy feeling gloom himself.

When I ask Mom why he's so cheerful, she says, "He's just got himself this weekend job at Eggplant and it has really put him in a good mood."

Eggplant is the local vegetarians' shop. Kurt himself is a vegetarian so he feels happy being surrounded by vegetables all day.

The only thing that can cheer me up is that Ruby Redfort is on TV tonight. I am utterly crazy about the Ruby Redfort books, as you may know, but unfortunately I am still waiting for Patricia F.

Maplin Stacey to write a new one, since I have read all the others at least maybe three times.

What's lucky is—and maybe you didn't know this—but they are now televised for the TV and they are on twice a week. There are loads of episodes, loads.

But it is not a new thing, the TV series. Mom says it was on in her day and they were made years ago, which is why the fashion looks a bit out of fashion.

They are re-showing it because Patricia F. Maplin Stacey has started writing books again and I'm sure they will be as popular as ever.

I didn't know all this information, but Betty looked it up on the website and told me. The new books will be quite different from the old ones and, I should think, more moderner.

Betty said, "Did you know she started writing the Ruby Redfort books way back, years and years ago in 1972?"—which was before most people were born.

The most exciting thing is that they are going to make Ruby Redfort into a movie.

Made by

HOLLYWOOD

Ruby is now thirteen and has this butler named Hitch, who wears a suit and is in the know about all her secret-agent work. He is very handsome and good-looking—my mom is quite sweet on him.

Ruby has a best friend called Clancy Crew, who is a boy who is very clever and also funny. They ride around together on bikes.

Betty and I know all the Ruby phrases—she says things like "Give me a break, bozo" and "Do you actually have a brain?"

You would be amazed if you know about Ruby Redfort because the Hollywood people will have to do all these gadgets and stuff. I am not sure how they will make them.

How do you make a walkie-talkie watch?

And roller skates that know which direction to go in if you say "Follow that car"?

And a purple helicopter that is bigger on the inside than on the outside?

The Ruby in the movie will be different from the one on the TV because the TV Ruby is now about almost at least forty years old, if not more.

She is named Jodie O'Neal and she is utterly brilliant even though she has blond hair when she is meant to have brown.

I bet Jodie O'Neal never had to worry about being good in a spelling bee.

❋ ❋ ❋